Justice & Love

Eva Sturm investigates her second case on Langeoog

An East Frisian crime story by Moa Graven

Imprint
Justice & Love
Eva Sturm investigates on Langeoog – The second case – East Frisian crime story by Moa Graven
All rights remain with the author
Translation in englisch by Nina Lochmann
Published in Criminal-kick-Verlag (East Frisia)
December 2017
ISBN 978-3-946868-29-3
Layout by Moa Graven

Content

Summer season on Langeoog is slowly approaching ist end. Eva Sturm already envisions herself spending long winter nights in front of the fire or at the little Italian place with Jürgen. But then the stamp club of East Frisia-Papenburg announces their arrival for a long weekend in October. And Jürgen of all people has gotten his hands on the supervision of this event and of course he instrumentalises Eva for his purposes. She is even supposed to deliver a speech during the gala dinner.

Things start to heat up when a collector wants to deposit a stack of valuable stamps with her. And then, after the dinner, Dieter Wattjes from Moormerland is lying lifeless on his hotel bed. Is jealousy or greed the motive for the brutal murder? And what role does a lawyer from Loga play in this charade?

Thank you!

I'd like to take this opportunity to thank the bunch of people who have stood by my side all this time I've been writing crime fiction. I have made many experiences, each and single one of which was precious in its own way!

I'd especially like to thank my darling for being so patient with me when I get immersed in days and nights of writing and become fairly unenjoyable for my surroundings.

While I was writing this novel, I have amassed quite some knowledge about the history of stamps. I'd like to express my gratitude in this respect the many clubs and their members for making an effort in carrying forth this knowledge.

Clouds over Langeoog

The skies would not tear up this morning. Dark clouds drew heavily across the horizon. Eva Sturm was still lying in bed and observed the spectacle through her bedroom window. She felt so lazy that she just could not bring herself to get out of bed. Summer was drawing to a close and she had a premonition this would be a long winter.

It would be her second. Last autumn she had been transferred to Langeoog. It felt like half an eternity to her. She had grown accustomed with the tardiness of East Frisia. In the afternoon she liked to have a cup of East Frisian tea with friends or by herself. Traditionally with some rock candy and a sip of cream that drew little clouds in the beverage. That tradition began to take its toll on her. Had she still been hoping in spring to be lying on the beach in her bathing suit in summer, she had now laid this dream to rest for the next few years. Because tea went so well with the little biscuits from her favourite bakery.

She struck her stomach and felt some unease. How was she supposed to lose those extra pounds? And the grey sky on top of that. How could anyone wonder that she preferred to stay in bed and draw the blanket over the tip of her nose. She peeked over to her alarm clock that displayed nine o'clock. She had to get a grip, no matter how little she felt like it. She had a standing appointment with Jürgen of the tourist office for a first informal meeting. And the subject of this meeting was at least as boring as the weather. Stamp collectors had actually chosen their island for a convention. And Jürgen, who had gotten supervision over this event, had asked her for support. Stamps of all things, Eva thought. How would anyone still make the effort of collecting those? True, as a young girl collecting stamps had been a common thing. Her parents used to have albums full of stamps. But she had never been able to comprehend what was so intriguing about that.

There was no use. She beat herself out of bed and took it to the bathroom. In the fridge there was nothing but cheese starting to curl up at the edges and a litre of milk. When had she gone grocery-shopping the last time? What was wrong with her? Was those menopause kicking in early? That was the last thing she needed. She poured herself a mug of coffee and chewed on a slice of crispbread that had lost most of its crispiness already. When she looked out of the window, the blanket of clouds had become denser. Every fibre of her body refused to get out there. But Jürgen was waiting. That was her only motivator right now.

»Good morning«, she said as shortly after she entered the tourist office.

»Hello, Eva«, Jürgen replied. »Tell me, are you moving to Sweden?«

»Why so?«

»Well, the way, you're dressed, you could make your way up to the North Pole. Are you really that cold?«

Eva made a disapproving gesture. »That's coming from the inside.«

Jürgen did not react to that. When women were bothered by something that came from deep within, man better not asked further questions. It would inevitably lead to discussions where he would lose in the long term, because he would not get the hang of it. It had been the same with his parents. And with many couples who came on holiday to the island, he witnessed it as well when they went their separate ways for days on the beach. He did not feel like getting into that.

»I hope you're on no deadline«, he said in high spirits. »Coffee and fresh breakfast rolls with cheese are awaing you.«

The smell had instantly gotten to Eva when she had stepped through the door.

»That sounds agreeable«, she forced herself to reply. She knew he meant well. And it was not his fault she felt so melancholic.

The two of them sat down at the visitors' table.

»There's a lot of work in organising such a spectacle. Had I known that before, I would've never gotten into that.«

The president of the stamp club had asked him for assistance. This fall the members of East Frisia-Papenburg had decided to convene on a nice East Frisian island and their choice had come to Langeoog.

»What's bothering you about that?«, Eva asked and took a bite off her cheese roll.

»Oh, I don't know. The phone keeps ringing, people keep registering and cancelling. This time the cat has died, the other time some grandmother needs to be committed to a retirement facility.«

»That bad?«, Eva murmured and slurped her coffee. Being pampered like that was soothing. She considered having breakfast with Jürgen every morning.

»Those guys are bordering on senility. Who in their right mind has a thing for stamps?«

»Maybe if there was an app for that«, Eva snickered.

»Oh, those young people...« Jürgen put a stack of papers in order that was lying in front of him on the table. »These are faxes and email print-outs«, he sighed. »If things keep going like this I'll need a new file just for that event.«

»Poor baby«, Eva grinned. She felt excellent.

»Keep laughing. I'm sitting here with that crap...«

»Come on... What can I do to help you?«

»It would be great if you could take care oft he accommodation«, Jürgen said placably. »I have put a list together for you. There are people who at all costs don't want to stay in a hotel with this and that participant.«

»I have heard that clubs are not as peacefully a place as they might suggest.« Eva was in high spirits and grapped for another cheese roll. She did not bother her figure or pounds, food tasted better in company. »How many rooms do you need?«

Jürgen scratched his head. »At that point I've got sixty-eight registrations, but there are couples involved. But here, I've made a list to clear it up for you.« He handed her a few sheets of paper.

Eva studied the names. None rang a bell.

»Okay, I'll get to it. Does this say how long the whole charade lasts?«

»It does«, Jürgen pointed with his fingertip on page one. »From October the ninth to eleventh.«

»Three days? Well, they must have some kind of programme then. Won't you have to make a reservation at a restaurant?«

»Right. Saturday night definitely. There is a Ja stimmt. Auf jeden Fall für den Samstagabend. There'll be a joint dinner. I've already taken care of that. They'll be eating at *Nordseehotel Kröger* at *Restaurant Verklicker*.«

»That doesn't sound too bad«, Eva said, who liked to eat at that restaurant. »And there'll be a lot of people to accommodate at the Kröger. I'll see how far I can get today.«

»Thank you, you're a great help.«

Eva heard it from Jürgen's register that there would be a lot of more work coming her way.

»But that's not all, right?«

»Well, there's one more thing... there are some members who own especially precious stamps which need to be stored safely.«

Eva rolled her eyes. She had suspected something like that. But she did not even have a strong box at the police station. Where should she put those?

»I don't know if that's a good idea«, she remarked. »I can hardly store those in my old tea box. There is no safe at the police station.«

»There isn't?«

Eva shook her head.

»That's unfortunate. But I've alreade assured the president that you'll take care of their treasures. What do we do now?«

Eva shrugged. »What about putting them with the bank?«

»Too much trouble. And I would have to explain to the president that the Langeoog police can't even secure a bunch of stamps. Do you want that to happen?« He made an embarrassed face. He had not meant to put Eva in that position.

»Well, at least you're coming clean now«, Eva murmured. »I'll try to get support from our Aurich branch. Maybe they can help me out with a safe for the time. I hope you haven't agreed on more obstacles for me in your alacrity, or...«

»No, that's about it. Well, I'd require your presence during the gala dinner. I've promised that much.«

»What? I'm supposed to spend the whole night by the side of drooling elderly gentlemen? Have you lost it? Why would you do that?«

Eva had jumped up in anger. She did not feel like doing that at all. What would she be talking about with those people? Jürgen had clearly shot it out of the ballpark this time.

Preparations

She had gotten the last single room at *Nordseehotel Kröger* and hung up. There would be a big event on Langeoog this weekend, the receptionist had apologised. She herself preferred to rent a double room whenever she travelled, even if she went alone. Or rather especially then, you never knew whom you ran into at the hotel bar. Dumb Dora. But Eva had pulled herself together and joined in with her chatterbox tone.

Everything went according to plan. The weekend mid-October was hers and her cold scheme. Everything was planned down to the last detail. The trap only had to snap.

In a good mood she put on the kettle and jumped under the shower. Then she rubbed herself down and took a glance in the mirror. He would regret having treated her like that.

During breakfast she read the paper but she could not quite focus. Would he bring his wife? She knew that she did not care for stamps. But whenever the club had a convention there was always the imminent danger of her coming. That would interfere with her well thought-out plan. She had to think of something. How easily a cyclist was overlooked by an approaching car. A broken wrist or ankle would surely keep her home. But there was a lot to do first. And she had a month time for her preparations.

She looked at her watch. She would have to hurry. Her first client would be here in half an hour. It was a man whose wife signed up for divorce shortly before their 25th anniversary. He would be losing his company too. That bothered him the most. A typical man, she thought. What guy knew a woman's worth these days? Her long blood-red nails dug into her left arm. Scraped the skin until they drew blood. She did not even feel it. Her desire for revenge was so powerful that she did not notice anything around her anymore.

One week later she sat in her dining-room, a grin covered her face. She read a notice of the Moormerland police. *Woman hit by car. Survived with heavy haematomas and a broken arm.* Sabine Wattjes would hardly accompany her husband to the convention on Langeoog.

Pizza with double cheese

Jürgen had surely meant well when he had given her the book on stamps and their history. But now she slammed the volume against the wall. She did not care if the black *One Penny* was the first stamp ever stuck on a letter. Or that that thing had no prongs.

Maybe her edginess was due to the weather. Since fall had ensued the wind was twirling around the houses. The tourist waves had receded and the hotels and restaurants were looking at the next run of pensioners and married couples who travelled aside from the school holidaysOb ihre Gereiztheit am Wetter lag? Seitdem es Herbst war, fegte der Wind um die Häuser. Der Touristenrummel war vorbei und die Hotels und Restaurants freuten sich schon auf den nächsten Ansturm der Rentnerpaare und Eheleute ohne Kinder, die gerne außerhalb der Ferien reisten. That was another type of people, a restaurant owner had once told her. They did not look on money and paid a lot for meals. No wonder. What family of five could afford a five-star restaurant?

Eva did not care about all of that now. In one week the collectors would invade. The police in Aurich had actually provided her with a safe, so she could safely put away the most valuable stamps. Her colleagues had made fun of her. Was there nothing more to do on the island put looking after paper snippets? They would like her job. Jackasses. Eva went to the living-room and threw herself on the sofa.

She had neglected her book on elves and fairies. She had meant to finish it that winter and then... what then? She had shown the first few chapters to her old friend Klara Bertschoo in Esens, who had been quite taken with it. There are hidden talents everywhere, she had told Eva. Obviously, being a police inspector did not count among them anymore, Eva thought and pressed a pillow against her face. See and hear nothing. The doorbell rang. Who might this be on a Sunday afternoon? She pulled herself up and went down the hallway.

Jürgen was standing in front of her. That was the last she needed. She had preferred not to see him for the next couple of days.

»What happened?«, she asked irritated.

»Can't I come over without something happening?«, Jürgen asked offended.

»I'm the police after all.«

»Are you angry?«

She suddenly felt bad. How he was standing there. It was not his fault she felt more twisted every day.

»Oh, I don't know. Everything's getting to me these days.«

»I was just dropping by for a coffee. You've gone off stage lately.«

Jürgen had noticed that she had not taken a step into the tourist office.

»I've read your book«, she said and led the way to the kitchen.

»I can see that.« Jürgen's gaze wandered to the floor where it lay before the cupboard.

»It fell down«, Eva murmured. She was aware that Jürgen had seen through her. »Well, I wasn't innocent in that matter«, she gave in and grinned.

Her foul mood lightened and both of them broke into laughter. That felt quite good.

»Thanks for coming over«, Eva finally said. »I've been running in circles lately. Please take a seat, I'll brew some coffee.«

»So your bad mood has nothing to do only with me and the stamp friends, that's reassuring«, Jürgen figured and sat down at the kitchen table.

»No«, Eva agreed. »But I can't tell you why I've been so irritated lately. Everything is just summing up I guess.«

» This might be your first island breakdown.«, Jürgen reasoned. »You've been living here for almost a year now. For a girl from Brunswick you've made it a long way.«

»Do you really think so?«

»I do. Living on an island is not that easy. The feeling of being cut off... Many don't go through with that in the long run.«

»I don't know... Things aren't so bad here after all.«

»That often is subconscious. You're feeling miserable and you don't know why. But i hope that won't make you burn some bridges. Because that goes away. Or so I've heard.«

»It could be the islanders.« Eva gave a serious expression and Jürgen's face dropped. »Hey, I was kidding. – So, what are you here for?«

»A cuppa, what else? There's not much going on in the office and Anja kann take care of that little traffic herself.«

»Anja? A new temp again?«

»Yes. She's a student trying to make a few bucks on the side.«

»And you still to waste your time with an old hag like myself?«

Jürgen refused from replying. He might as well walk through Iraq dressed as Uncle Sam.

»How do you feel about Italian tonight?«, he asked instead.

»Good thinking«, Eva agreed. Another pizza would not do her figure any additional harm.

After coffee Jürgen went back to the office and they set a date for seven p.m.

Eva made use of the remaining time to clean up the kitchen. When they was all sweaty and the kitchen gleamed they was sure she was getting old. Why else would she be cleaning like a lunatic on a Sunday? Those were usually women who were old, fat and spinsters. Dammit. She threw the rag into the basin. That would be the last time she was doing that, she swore. And if mold was closing up to the ceiling, she would not become one of them.

She went to the bedroom, took off her tracksuit she would always wear when she had a day off and went for a shower. Jürgen was not the worst option. He was her minor. Maybe she should feel flattered that he was coming on to her. It had been like that from day one. But so far, she had always growled at him like an angry old dog. Why? Actually, she found him quite nice and good-looking. She even felt a slight attraction. But still she pushed him away when he complimented her. Was she really that deranged? She kept grinding on that while the drops were raining down on her. That was it. She was old. She looked down herself, even though she usually tried not to do that. Hesitatingly she touched her stomach. And soon she would be eating a pizza again. Even if Jürgen did not see her right now – God bless – her physical condition was easy to guess even if she was dressed. He was no idiot. Of course he knew she carried some extra pounds. And a big rack. But did that appal him? No.

But she was sure that he would only see her in her birthday suit when there was a complete lunar eclipse. She was scared of him seeing her naked. She lathered herself up again and put the tab on boil, then on freeze and then turned it off and left the shower. She was ridiculous. But she knew many women had to feel like that. She had to work on her self-esteem. The next weekend surely would not work in her favour.

Jürgen did not suspect any of her dark thoughts and greeted her heartily when she arrived at the pizza parlour.

»Looking good«, he remarked and handed her the menu.

»You sound surprised«, Eva said with slight anger in her voice. Could she for one do without the bitchy retorts? She would work on that. Quite a task.

Jürgen rolled his eyes and scanned the dishes as if he would go for anything else than usually. So pizza with salami, ham and double cheese it was.

»I've ordered a bottle of Chianti«, he remarked.

»I can use that today«, Eva said and looked for a lean pizza dish, which she of course did not find.

By the end of the night she was glad that Jürgen was there. The dropped her off at her doorstep and said farewell with a hug, probably due to the second bottle of Chianti and the complimentary Marsala. It felt good. They kept things at that stage.

Club Life

Dieter Wattjes poured another cup of tea. There was some time left until his colleague Freerk would pick him up. The two men would go to the convention by themselves. His wife had had a bicycle accident and her broken arm disabled her. She did not feel like going. The car's driver had committed a hit-and-run and the police still had not found him. Chances were getting slimmer from day to day. Freerk's wife had offered to stay in Moormerland with Sabine and help her with the chores. Sabine had declined. She knew how much Mathilde was looking forward to the convention. There was no better place for gossip.

»Got everything?«, Sabine asked her husband when she entered the kitchen.

»I think so. Freerk will be here in a bit.« He stirred his tea.

»Have fun«, Sabine said and sat down at the table.

»You could've come. A broken arm...« He did not get any further. Sabine cut him off with a strict gesture.

»Let it be. I don't mind. I'll hear about the latest club gossip early enough.« She herself did not collect stamps, like most wives of the club members. Like everywhere in the country men flocked together in some or another club and their wives were just decoration. She was actually glad to get out of that for a weekend. She intended to enjoy those three days in her own way.

»I think somebody has pulled up«, she said. Finally the house would be quiet.

The doorbell rang. Sabine opened.

Dieter grabbed his wallet and keys and put on his jacket.

After five minutes the door slammed shut. Sabine breathed deeply.

First she went into the kitchen and cleared the table. Then she opened every window for the fall wind to carry out the smell of beer and stuffiness. She was incredibly happy in this moment. Dieter did not suspect a thing. Of course he did not.

He was too busy thinking of himself. And that other woman. Did he really think she would not notice? He must have thought she was an idiot. They had been married for some time, fifteen years to be precise, but there was still some harmony left. They even had sex from time to time. Until one year ago when Dieter started to change. It came creeping. But for a sensitive woman's ears there were some signs, all those extra hours he started working. Dieter was the blueprint cheater. She started to go through his personal things. That was blueprint as well. She found receipts of bouquets. She would only get flowers for their anniversary. If he thought of it. For one year she had even gotten some for her birthday. Suspicious. But the flowers he bought in between, the receipts of which she had found, were out of range and not for her.

She was irritated how little she cared. The scarce occasions of matrimonial intercourse only occurred every other month. She did not miss it. Sometimes Dieter felt strange to her when he was reading his paper next to her at the breakfast table. Sometimes she wondered who that man was that was sitting next to her. Where had the timid young man gone who had picked her up in his first Opel?

Their marriag had remained childless. That would be an advante if they split up.

The apartment was cooling down. Sabine shut the windows. She took the post from the letter-box. It was only advertisements.

She took a look at her watch. It would be eleven soon. Dieter and Freerk would be already on the ferry to Langeoog. He had not cancelled the double room he had booked when he still thought she would be coming. Would he be taking her? The extra hours had diminished lately and she did not find any more proof of his unfaithfulness.

She went upstairs to the bedroom and took her suitcase from under the bed. She would soon know what Dieter was up to on Langeoog. Her ferry would leave in the afternoon.

On the ferry to Lageoog it was quite busy. Most passengers sat below deck and had already ordered the first shots. It would be three awesome days and they wanted to drink to that. The men were sitting together and were laughing loudly while their wives worried about children and broken dishwashers at the next table.

Some stood on deck, wrapped in thick coats and let the rough sea air blow around their noses. They were talking little and found it too stuffy and loud downstairs.

But they all had one thing in common. They all loved stamps and the sociable get-together among people of their kind. Many of them had brought their albums as there was a swapping event planned on Sunday morning.

When the ship anchored before Langeoog, Eva and Jürgen were still awaiting them.

»There they are«, Eva hushed, »I can spot them from the old woollen hand-knit sweaters.«

»Pull yourself together«, Jürgen reproached laughing. »They are only people.«

He had agreed with the president that there should be a small reception after the arrival. Jürgen would give them a short overview over the sights of the island and Eva would tell about the possibility to store valuable stamps in the provided safe.

But when the group landed, everything came differently. They split into groups and looked for their hotels.

A tall elderly man walked towards Jürgen.

»Moin, I'm Wilfried Sievers, wir talked on the phone«, he presented himself and extended his hand.

»So much about our plan«, Jürgen said and followed the bags with his eyes.

»They are always like that«, the president chuckled. »They don't get out that much.«

Eva wondered if he meant that.

»How does your further schedule look like?«, Jürgen asked.

»We will be investigating the island and grab a bite to eat in the evening. The can travel in groups as they like before the big dinner tomorrow. There are always some cliques, you know.«

Jürgen nodded. »I can imagine. So I guess I can't do much for you. Maybe one or the other will find their way to my tourist office.«

»What about the safe for the precious stamps?«, Eva asked, even though they would have preferred to be far away.

»Tell your friends. We worry about security.«

»Already done. I announced it on the ferry. But so far nobody said anything. Maybe they left their babies at home.«

»I only meant to bring it to your attention.« Eva growled. »I'll be off then.« She gave the two men a nod and disappeared.

»She doesn't mean it«, Jürgen said.

»Jo«, the president agreed. »I'll be in my room.«

In Secret Mission

She had had a fresh salad, a glass of champahne and a bowl of strawberries brough to her room. If she wanted to keep her figure, that would have to suffice as lunch.

Now she was lying on her be in lace underwear and played with her toes in the satin sheets. Too bad she had no company. The atmosphere would have been ideal.

Her face darkened the next moment. Dieter was not that far away. And yet there was more distance between them than ever before. It stung her heart. Why had he broken up with her without warning? Had his wife come onto them? He had not said a word, only that they had to end it.

She had cried for three days and had not been able to go to the registry. It was her destiny that men could not imagine a lasting relationship with her. Even though she looked smashing. An immaculate body, long legs and wavy long hair that framed her mysterious eyes. But still she was always second in line. Most men with whom she entered a relationship were married. Were those men attracted by her because they were bored in their marriages or did she only fancy committed men whom she could not have for themselves because she herself had commitment issues? In early years she had tried to get to the ground of that with the help of a therapist whom she started to see because she had looked for solace in alcohol. That had scared her. She was a successful lawyer and still she was alone. Lonely.

Bothered by those thoughts she finally fell asleep.

Sabine Wattjes parked the car and looked around. If anyone would recognise her in her costume? She felt quite ridiculous with the dark wig. She had burst into laughter when she put it on at home. She was a natural blonde and did not recognise herself. But that had been her goal. Stay on the down-low. Only her plastered arm worried her. It was a welcomed justification not to go to the convention. She had never meant to go to the club meeting but instead spy on her husband. She needed to know her place. And when she was not there it was the perfect occasion for him to see his lover. She imagined the two between the sheets. It still hurt. Maybe she love Dieter a lot more than she allowed herself to think.

In order to cover up her arm she had bought a poncho from the internet. It had arrived in time and she was glad because the wind was freezing cold.

When she boarded the ferry she quickly got a nice place under deck. She kept the poncho on. Nobody should remember a woman with a plaster.

The Safe

Eva had just put her feet on her desk when the door opened.

»Good morning«, said a man whom she did not know.

»Is there a problem?« Eva took her feet of the table and sat up straight.

The stranger declined. »It's about my collection.«

Well, she thought, one of those creeps.

»You mean stamps?«

The man nodded. »I've heard I can deposit them here in a safe.«

»That's right. But only if it is a valuable piece. I can't have that safe overflow with worthless junk.«

The man pulled the door close behind him and bowed conspiringly over the desk. »I've got a very special stamp«, he whispered. »Nobody knows that I own it. I'll have this bomb detonate on Sunday at the swapping show. They won't believe their eyes.«

Eva stood up. The situation put her in unease. And that man had a bad case of haliatosis. »If you would hand me the precious then. I'll lock her up and put her to safety.«

The man looked around as if somebody were in the room. Then he pulled an envelope from his jacket.

»It's in here.« He handed Eva the envelope. It had a grease stain. There were crazy people out there.

»What's your name? I need to write you a receipt.« Eva took the envelope and carried it to the open safe as so far nobody has handed anything in. She let the door click close.

The man observed her with his mouth open. »I'm Heinrich Gerlach«, he said soundless.

»Well, Mr Gerlach.« Eva sat down and scribbled something on the receipt block. »I hereby assure the stamp has been placed with the Langeoog police. When would you like to pick it up? You said you need the stamp on Sunday. I'm usually not in the station on Sundays, so we'd have to make an appointment.«

The man looked at her sheepishly. Had he heard what she had said?

»Have you heard me, Mr Gerlach?«

»Yes yes...«, he murmured. »Sunday. I'll be back on Sunday morning.«

»At what hour? We need to fix a time. Eva began to get angry.

»Fix a time... yes yes.« The man was on his way out.

»Mr Gerlach, wait!«, Eva yelled.

He did not seem to hear her, then he opened the door and walked out into the darkness.

»That can't be happening«, Eva ranted to herself. She did not feel like running after him. Typical, those men from the country. If they were let loose. The way he behaved and smelled he was a farmer who lived by himself on an old ranch after his wife had died early. The worn-down corduroy pants he was wearing spoke in favour of that theory. No woman would let her man go out like that.

She did not feel like fussing around about that man. She was long off shift. She wondered that Jürgen had not given her notice. She was hungry. Why had he not called to ask her for dinner? She grabbed the phone and put it back instantly. Maybe it was a good idea to spend this night by herself in the apartment. She would have a hard day at the club dinner.

She put her things together and turned off the lights.

When she made a turn along the beach on the way home she thought she heard water splashing. As if someone was moving his hands quickly in the water. When she looked out onto the sea she could not make out much. The moon that lit up the rough sea was cover by dark heavy clouds. She could not see her hand before her eyes. And she did not feel like making inquiries now. Surely it had only been the wind mixing up the water. She should not interpret too much into that.

It was close to seven p.m when she arrived at her apartment. It was freezing cold. Had her radiator failed? She turned on the light and walked toward the heating room. Really, nothing worked. She had no choice but to call Jürgen.

»My heating broke down. It's freezing in here.«

»I thought you'd never call«, Jürgen laughed. »I'll be there in a bit.«

Had he been waiting for her call? She put down the phone.

A few grips and the heat returned to Eva's rooms.

»Thank you«, she said and meant it.

»Don't mention it. Have you eaten anything?«

»To be honest, my stomach is down to my knees«, Eva confessed. »I was just about to cook up something.«

»How about eating out?«, Jürgen asked.

»I don't know. The island is populated with these freaks. I don't feel like hearing any more about stamps.«

»To be honest, I'm done with them as well. Some of them came by the office. But they're not as bad. They told me some things I didn't know.«

»Have you ever missed not knowing that?« Eva could not stop teasing.

»Some extra knowledge doesn't hurt.«

»You can't measure intelligence.«

»Not everyone's«, Jürgen replied.

Now both had to laugh heartily. Eva could finally take off her jacket because it was snug and cozy in her apartment again.

»Have a seat in the living-room and turn on the TV. I'll make some fried eggs on rye«, she said.

»Do you have a cold one for us?«, Jürgen asked.

»Of course, take out some glasses.«

They watched a crime programme and Eva figured out after ten minutes who was the culprit. But that did not matter now. It was nice to be sitting there with Jürgen, grab a bite and feel the togetherness.

»By the way«, she said abruptly. »Someone put something in the safe today.«

»Only one? I had reckoned with more«, Jürgen wondered.

»He was a creep. Some Mr Gerlach. He deposited a greasy enveloped which was supposed to contain a precious stamp.«

»Did you have a look?«

»No, I didn't care much. He wanted to get it back for the swapping thing on Sunday. But when I tried to make an appointment, he didn't even react.«

»Maybe you were just talking past each other.«

Eva took a sip of her beer and shook her head. »No, really, he was strange. Like he was barely listening.«

»Well, try not to care. They'll be gone on Sunday and we'll have our peaceful island back.«

»I can't wait«, Eva said and carried the dirty dishes into the kitchen.

Jürgen and she had another beer and he bid farewell at eleven p.m.

On his way home he walked past a pub where there was quite some traffic. People laughed and talked loudly. He pressed his nose against the glass and noticed a merry round of men and tables full of beer and shot glasses. They surely belonged to the club. Should he go in? Why not, he thought. He was not tired at all and he could to with a shot.

The Shadow

Sabine was freezing while she was observing the entrance of *Nordseehotels Kröger* from a secluded perspective. It was short before one a.m. and Dieter had still not returned. Had she missed him? No, she was sure he was still roaming about town. Probably he was sitting in some pub with his mates, downing some beers, while she was sheepishly waiting here. What had she been thinking? At that time of the year. The only upside was that is darkened early. She pressed harder against the boxwood hedge to shelter from the breeze. If anyone saw her they had to think she was crazy. Almost one thirty. Even if Dieter now retreated to the hotel, he could barely satisfy another woman. She pulled her poncho tighter to keep the cold from creeping in.

She almost was ready to walk back to her hotel when a dark figure approached the place. Was it Dieter? No, that was no man. In the faint light of the entrance she made out a tall slim woman with a dark trench-coat and had a big scarf wrapped around her head. She was wearing shades.

In the middle of the night? Was she the woman her husband was cheating with? Was she on her way to their joint love nest to await him?

Her pulse was racing. She felt no cold. She knew Dieter's room number was 214. If the room lit up now, she would have security. She waited. Three minutes... four minutes... after ten minutes she knew had had erred. The woman had not entered his room. But that was only a vague comfort. She might as well have her own room in the hotel.

Frustrated and frozen to the core, Sabine walked back to her hotel half an hour later. The next night she would have to be smarter to catch her husband in the act. She could not know that Dieter had retreated to his room at eight and pulled the blanket over his nose and was sleeping the sleep of the just. And so he did not notice when someone knocked on his door at one in the morning.

The Precious Stamp

On Saturday morning Eva was long awake before her alarm clock rang at eight. Today was the big day for the stamp lot. Jürgen had asked her to make a little speech. And so she had not been able to sleep for two hours. What would she be saying? She did not have the faintest idea. Frustrated, she got out of bed, put on the kettle and walked into the bathroom. Suddenly she did not feel like sitting in her kitchen all by herself. That would make her loneliness all too obvious. So she refrained from showering, did with brushing her teeth, made a face at her own reflection and took it to the living-room to get her laptop. Then she got the coffee and crawled back into her sheets.

Via *Wikipedia* she dived into the world of philatelists.

After sifting through some pages she was stunned that all of that had gone past her so far. Considering the stamps' history as the main mean for transport of letters, she had to admit, there was some attraction to it. She dreamed of owning the first stamp, the *One Penny Black* from the United Kingdom of 1840 and to impress the club members tonight. She wondered what treasure Mr Gerlach owned. She was getting curious. Maybe she should go to the station and have a peak? Maybe later, she thought, and copied some information from the internet into a new document to print it out for her speech later.

She was so immersed into her research that she did not even realise it was already ten when her doorbell rang. She had agreed to meet Jürgen for a coffee in the beach café but only in the afternoon. She let it ring and kept browsing the inernet. The first official stamp of 1840 was rather a paper strip without an adhesive back. It had to be attached to the letter with a clip. In Germany the *Schwarze Einser (Black One)* was the first stamp in 1849. At some point the glue area was introduced as well as the perforation to improve easy handling.

Eva was divided. She had not imagined this to be so intriguing. She had hated History back in school. Eva war hin und her gerissen. Dass das Thema so spannend sein konnte, hätte sie nie gedacht. Schon in der Schule war ihr das Geschichtsfach ein Graus gewesen. But now that it had entered the real life it had some interest to it. She looked at her clock. It was almost then thirty. She could not stop to think about the envelope in her safe. She had to know its content. She put away her blanket and went to the bathroom.

Half an hour later Eva turned the numer dial on the safe. She opened the lid carefully as if she was doing somethink forbidden. There it was, the greasy envelope. Should she? Yes. Now that she was here, she wanted to know. She sat down at her desk and opened the envelope. But instead of a stamp she found a torn piece of paper with shaky writing:

Please don't look for me. Life has lost all meaning. My Stella is dead and the farm is close to ruin. Tell my children I'm sorry. Heinrich Gerlach, October of 2015

Holy shit, Eva thought after reading this for the fifth time. A suicide note. Eva already saw the headlines. She was sure Gerlach had killed himself. That was what this was: a suicide note. She remembered the splashing sound from last night. Had this idiot drowned himself right before her eyes? Could she have prevented his death? She considered putting the letter back. Only Jürgen knew that

Gerlach had made a deposit. She could easily shut him down. She remembered that darn receipt she had given to Gerlach. She had only one chance, she had to find his body before anyone else did and traced his last steps back to her station. With that storm the body might have been carried out into the wild. If it stayed out two days the receipt would dissolve, at least the ink would disappear. She was thinking like a con already. She felt ashamed. But after those years on the job the mind played cruel jokes.

She grabbed the phone and called Jürgen. »You have to come ASAP«, she said and hung up.

»You can't just throw this out«, Jürgen yelled after reading it. »What's wrong with you? Someone took his own life and you want to cover it up?« He looked at her flustered.

»Jürgen, you have to see that in a pragmatic way«, Eva said coldly. »How will it look when this comes out? And if anyone finds out that I was the last to see him, they will wonder why I didn't notice anything.«

»I've been wondering that too.«

»See? I'd only like thinks to even out.«

»You've lost your mind«, Jürgen complained. »Eighty club mates will be expecting Gerlach at dinner. Do you really think nobody will wonder where he is? Are you really that naive?« Jürgen kept shouting and Eva drew back. What this the end of their good relationship?

»You're right«, she finally agreed. »Maybe it's just my bad conscience. I could've prevented a suicide.«

»What? This is getting better by the minute...«

»When I was walking home last night I heard strange sounds. But I thought it would be the wind in the water.« She made a resentful face.

Jürgen calmed down. »I will just forget what you've proposed. We'll call the coast guard and tell them that a man is missing. Agreed?«

Eva nodded and typed the number. Then they walked tot Nordseehotel to inform the presidennt. Of course news got around quickly and many were standing at the beach of Langeoog. It was like in Eva's worst nightmares. Of course the local journalist took photos and interviewed club members. The dinner would be no fun at all.

The Big Dinner

Dieter Wattjes could have sworn he knew those long legs he had spotted, shortly before the elevator door closed. Because he did not want to wait he took the stairs. In the last moment Sabine could take refuge in a storage room when Dieter came her way. When had he ever used the stairs? He surely had not noticed her with the black her and the shades. But her heard was beating through her throat when she heard him pass her.

The mood was subtle when Dieter entered *Restaurant Verklicker*. Almost everyone was there. But she celebrational atmosphere had made way fort he sadness of a lost club mate who had chosen to leave this life.

Eva curled up her print-out. Nobody wanted to hear today what she was thinking of collecting stamps.

The president praised Heinrich Gerlach's friendly nature and his commitment for the club. Of course, now they were all on common terms that the deceased was the carrying pillar of the institution. They clinked glasses even though they had not even found the body.

Eva imagined how the door opened and Gerlach entered slightly confused. But she did not quite believe for that to happen. So she downed another korn. Jürgen was sitting next to her and had obviously still not gotten over her trying to suck him into a vicious conspiracy.

Eva nudged him.

»What?«

»I'm sorry.«

»Hm ...«

»Jürgen?« The alcohol made her lower her boundaries.

»What?« He turned towards her.

»Can you... forgive me?« Her eyes became wet.

Jürgen saw it in the lighting. He felt sorry for her.

»It's alright. Let's forget about it.« He held another korn in front of her.

»I'll never do it again, promise«, she mumbled into his collar.

»You better, or I'll have to put you over my knee«, Jürgen grinned.

She smiled and poured another.

Short before midnight the first guests staggered out of the restaurant. Heinrich Gerlach had been sent of accordingly and the dinner had been widely appreciated. At some point the atmosphere had loosened up due to the consumption of alcohol and some began to crack jokes. Club life went on.

Eva and Jürgen left the party and went along the beach where Eva had to throw up. Then she hooked into Jürgen who took her to the apartment.

»Do you want a coffee?«, Eva asked sobered up when they were standing in front of her door.

»Not today«, Jürgen said. »I have to get up early.«

He said goodbye with a breathy kiss on the cheek and went his way.

Around one Wattjes was fed up as well. He took the short way from the toilet to the elevator to go to his hotel room. Nothing had connected him with Gerlach, the old man meant nothing to him. He had preferred to have a good time. At that moment, it was a pity that Sabine had broken her arm. Maybe it would have been a good opportunity to spend another nice night outside of your own four walls.

But now he stood alone in front of his room door. Inside, he first took a look in the minibar. After champagne and red wine he did not mind. But there was also a vial of coastal fog in it. He unscrewed the lid and downed the schnapps. It was burning in his throat. He threw himself on the bed. His eyes almost closed when he suddenly thought he heard a noise.

Was someone knocking on his door? He straightened up and pricked up his ears. Indeed. Someone was there. He turned from the bed and opened.

The Sunday After

Sabine Wattjes had red-rimmed swollen eyes, which she hid behind sunglasses. She was now on the first ferry to Bensersiel. She had been crying all night. Until she fell asleep. The realization that she had been right in her assumption had been both relieving and sad at the same time.

She did not sit down under the deck, though the sun was overcast by dark clouds. She punished herself with the whipping cold wind that ran down her skin like a sharp knife. She wanted to feel pain. Other than those in her heart. Because they hurt much more. What would she do first, when she was back home in Moormerland? Cleaning? Cook? Shop? It seemed absurd to continue her life as before. Should she just pack her things and disappear? To be gone without a trace? But she knew she could not do that. She was the type of woman who needed to talk about everything. She needed clear circumstances, even if they hurt. She could not live with a man who betrayed her. But she was not naive either. The fifteen years of marriage had not been easy for her either. Who could sustain the feeling of falling in love in the long run? She too had flirted with other men. Only, as far as she had never gone. Would it be easier if she too had a relationship? But what was a marriage worth if you were not loyal to the other? Many men of her friends were not loyal. This was a regular topic during the afternoon tea and cake in the neighborhood. Sabine liked to think of it. She wanted to believe in love, not in something that passed. She loved Dieter. Why could he do that to her? Tears ran down her cheeks again and burned on the ice-cold skin. Now a light rain started. She decided to go down to the deck and have a coffee. Her hands felt dead.

"Sorry," said a voice beside her. Sabine did not even look up. Someone had jostled her. She did not care. If she had raised her eyes she might have recognized her. But so she went down with her head bowed past her.

On Langeoog, the first members of the club slowly made their way to the group room in the Nordseehotel. Many still grumbled about the many schnapps skulls. At eleven o'clock it should start with the exchange. After a lunch in the hotel restaurant, the first people in the afternoon wanted to go back to the ferry again because they had to work again the next day.

"How are you?" Eva asked as she opened the door to the tourist information.

Jürgen looked up in surprise. "So early on your feet?" He asked, ignoring her question.

The mood was clearly still overcooled.

"Are not there cheese rolls today?" Eva asked, laughing. Jürgen had to be thawed somehow.

"No, we were not dating today," Jürgen said shortly.

Old stubborn ass, Eva thought.

"Well, I'll go to the office," Eva said finally, ignoring her. But before she could go out the door, it was torn open from the outside.

"There's a dead man in the North Sea Hotel," a young woman shouted. "You must come immediately, Eva."

Eva knew her by reputation. "At the hotel?" She asked in disbelief, for she remembered Heinrich Gerlach immediately. But how was he supposed to have come to the hotel? His room had been empty when people had been looking for him. And since she thought she had gone into the water, it was unlikely he was dead in the hotel now.

"Yes, there is blood everywhere. The boss said I should look for you ... because I did not meet you at the office ... "She was breathing heavily with excitement.

"Okay, let's go now," Eva said and left with her. Jürgen followed them. His curiosity was clearly greater than his hurt feelings.

"His name is Dieter Wattjes," the young woman said as she ran beside Eva.

"The dead?"

The young woman nodded. "I wanted to make the beds this morning, so I spotted him. It was so terrible. "

It worked feverishly in Eva's head. First a suicide and then murder. And all this here on her small island at a club meeting. She hoped that was really the last bad news before the group left again on Monday.

The hotel was in a state of excitement. Many club members were gathered in the foyer and whispered together. Just the women stood together and nodded to each other and put their hands over their mouths.

"Mrs. Sturm, good that you come," the hotel owner said. "I locked the room so nobody would go in there."

"That was a good decision," Eva praised. "What room number?"

"I'll take you there." The hotelier led the way to the elevator.

Dieter Wattjes lay half-clothed on his stomach on his bed. The pillow with his head in an unnaturally twisted posture was dyed deep red. Obviously, somebody had given him one neat one.

"Please leave me alone now," Eva said. "There should not be too many people in there before the forensics was there."

"Of course." The hotelier retreated.

Meanwhile, Jürgen talked to the chairman of the stamp club in the hotel lobby.

"These are really sad circumstances under which your event takes place here," he said sympathetically.

"Well, we'll all just forget that," said the chairman. "And somebody has to have Sabine, too ... I'll inform Dieter's wife. She actually wanted to be there, but she had an accident and stayed at home. Good thing they do not have kids. "

"Yes, when children are affected, it's always twice as bad. How well did you know the victim? "

"The Dieter? Oh, I've known him for over ten years when he joined our club. He was a fine guy. No fly has done any harm. I do not understand any of this ..."

"So you have no idea who might have killed him?" Jürgen asked. Then he was rudely pulled back on the sleeve.

"Do you have a witness interview here?" Eva hissed at him.

"I just wanted to help you ..."

"You know that will enable me to get into the devil's kitchen ..."

"You're feeling very well," said Jürgen snappishly.

"Now it's really enough. We will talk later."

Eva turned away before she spit out any more malice.

When she turned around, the club chairman had disappeared from her sight.

Half an hour later, forensics arrived from Aurich. Also forensic scientist Ole Meemken had flown over. When Dieter Wattjes was carried outside in a zinc coffin, Eva sat down with Ole Meemken at a table in the restaurant.

"The skull of the victim has burst like a ripe melon," the coroner said.

Eva had to choke. Which might have been the grain she had poured into her last night, like mineral water.

"What could have been the murder weapon," she said between her teeth.

"Hm ... definitely something damn heavy," said Ole Meemken. "For such a force, a bottle of wine is not enough. Because otherwise I have not found anything else in the room, which would be in question. But as I said, it must have been something else. "

"Maybe the culprit took the murder weapon," Eva suggested.

"That's what I'm expecting. And maybe he had brought her too. "

"That would mean intent."

Ole Meemken nodded. "When I have completed the final examination, I will send you the report immediately."

"OK. And please check if he had sex. "

"I always do," laughed Meemken, "men who live alone in hotel rooms are quite capable of doing that."

"Yes sorry. I meant only because he lay half naked on the bed. "

"All right."

As the crowds in the hotel slowly dissolved, because there was nothing more interesting to see, Eva discovered that Jürgen was sitting alone at a table in the foyer. She ran over to him when he spotted her.

"What crap, right?" She sat down beside him.

"Can you say ... and I had everything so well prepared." Jürgen really seemed bent. He was least of all blamed for everything.

"I feel a little idle now. Shall we go to the Italian together? "

Jürgen nodded and they left the hotel after Eva told the chairman that she was expecting all the members of the association at 3 pm for a questionnaire in the hotel restaurant.

Today Eva also ordered a pizza with double cheese. In addition a large bottle of mineral water. She had some after-burn.

"I'm so glad when they all leave tomorrow," she moaned when she had half eaten.

"Never again a stamp club on Langeoog," complained Jürgen. "Certainly not with my support."

"Now stop it. You did your job well. But I wonder what's behind the murder. "She wiped her mouth with a napkin. "Did this Wattjes have a valuable stamp?"

"You mean, he was hit on the head for a piece of paper?"

"Oh, you have no idea what these things are worth. I'm more into it. There are stamps worth millions. "

"Oh, and you think that of all things an East Frisian has brought such a treasure to Langeoog in his carry-on? Would not he have taken your safe then? "

Eva thought for a moment. "You're right. Even if it was not about millions, but he would have brought them to safety. Then all that remains is jealousy. "

"Or rivalries within the club."

"Or all together," Eva said. "Anyway, I'll have to go over to the mainland tomorrow and ask Dieter Wattjes's wife. Two officers from the mainland are already on their way to deliver the bad news to her. "

"Then I'll come with you," said Jürgen.

"As? To Moormerland to Mrs. Wattjes? "

"I agree."

"But why? And besides, you have your tourist information. "

"Oh, Anja can do it alone. I've got something to make up for you. "He glanced at his plate.

"That's rubbish. You acted right when you stopped me from this unspeakable plan. I must have completely lost my mind for a moment. "

"One moment, well ..." Jürgen said. Everything was the same again, Eva thought contentedly. Secretly she was glad that Jürgen would accompany her.

"I'm sorry I hit you so much in front of the club chairman," she said, her mouth full.

"Nevermind. You're right, you're the investigator here, "Jürgen said. "It was banter anyway. They've known each other for over ten years, but he did not say anything about a particularly valuable stamp. And I suppose that at least the club chairman would know if the Wattjes had such a thing. "

"Well, you see, that'll take us a long way," Eva said, satisfied.

At exactly three o'clock Eve returned to the hotel and unbuttoned each club member individually. When she finished the questioning, it was almost eight o'clock. And it had not taken her any further. Everyone was horrified, could not explain anything and hoped that they caught the culprit. And nobody could imagine that Dieter Wattjes had been killed because of a love affair.

And that he should have particularly valuable stamps, no, no one had ever heard of that.

Back Home

When she came to her apartment, she first took off her thick shoes. She was not used to running around in such blocks. But since she did not assume that stiletto heels were unremarkable enough on an East Frisian island in October, she had taken boots with her. And she had not looked back. It was damn cold on the way back. And then it had started to rain too.

She put her bag in the guest room, stripped off her trench coat, and slid it carelessly onto the thick carpet.

In the kitchen she took a bottle of champagne from the fridge and poured herself a glass. The tingling on her tongue reminded her of last night. He had been so hot on her. He had whispered the most obscene words in her ear again and again by the alcohol, so that her neck was a single erogenous zone with tiny little hairs set up. No, she had not had such good sex in a long time. She was sure he had felt the same way.

Elated she ran into the bathroom and let water run into the round tub. She wanted to relax and then prepare the documents for the first clients the next day.

As Sabine Wattjes drove up the driveway, she felt a sense of desolation. Paralyzed, she sat in her car. She could not get out now and go to the house that belonged to them together. The dream of married life was over forever. She would never again be able to trust him. Never again. Did it rain or was it her tears that veiled her eyes? Her hands clenched the steering wheel so that it hurt.

Suddenly someone knocked on the windowpane.

"Mrs. Wattjes? Is everything ok?"

That was the neighbor next door. Ironically, the woman who stuck to the windowpane all day and probably knew more about her life than she did. She could not possibly see her in that state. The next day the whole street would know that she had sat in front of the house in her car, her eyes red-rimmed. And that she was a very pitiable woman.

Sabine did not answer. She pushed the doorknob down, started the car again, and drove off the driveway. Out of the corner of her eye, she saw the neighbor jump back, startled. Even with her feet crossed, she did not care at the moment.

Sabine did not know how long and where she had gone. Finally she stood in Emden in a large parking lot. She looked in the rearview mirror. The swelling of the eyes had gone down a little. Could she dare sit in a cafe? Why not, she thought, and got out. Who should know her here? She rarely went to Emden, and relatives did not exist either. So she found a free table in a nice restaurant and ordered a pot of coffee. She wanted to wait until it was dark before she drove home again. Home, she thought. Did that have any meaning at all?

As she stirred and pondered in her coffee, her neighbor answered questions from two officers who had rung her doorbell. Yes, she has already seen Ms. Wattjes today, said the neighbor. She had behaved somehow strange. Have sat on their driveway in their car and did not get out. When she knocked on her window to inquire if everything was alright, she just gasped and bolted. Did something happen? The officials said nothing about the murder of Dieter Wattjes. They only told the neighbor that she should inform her immediately if Sabine Wattjes reappeared. The neighbor, contrite, inserted the business card and promised to call. With a pot of tea and a few slices of bread with lard and grease she made herself comfortable at her kitchen window and waited.

When Sabine drove to her driveway at seven o'clock, the door in the adjoining house was torn open impatiently.

"Mrs. Wattjes ... wait," the neighbor called excitedly and came running over.

Such a mess, Sabine thought. Why could not that person just leave her alone?

"The police were there," the neighbor gasped out of breath as she stood in front of Sabine.

"The police?" Sabine was listening. "Why? What did you want from me? "

"I do not know that. But I have a card with the number where you should call. That is, you actually asked me to call you if they came back home. But you can actually

even ..."

She handed the card to Sabine.

"Thank you. Then I'd better get in touch with you, "Sabine said and started to go inside.

The neighbor stood there rooted to the spot. Of course, Sabine knew that now she wanted to know everything as a reward. But she herself did not know what it was all about and would certainly not trust this person.

"Thanks again for your help," Sabine said and disappeared into the house. When she looked out the corridor window, the neighbor had disappeared.

She put down her bag and took off her jacket and shoes. She was so tired and exhausted. She wanted to take a bath now and just crawl into bed. But what did the police want from her? It was certainly her duty to get in touch now. Even at this time.

So she picked up the phone and dialed the number on the business card. A Mathias Sanders from the police station in Leer answered. When he knew who he was dealing with, he explained that he would come soon.

Funny, Sabine thought. It must have happened something worse.

Half an hour later, she fainted in her living room.

Eva and Jürgen in Moormerland

"You know Jürgen, I think it's nice that you always accompany me, but that's how I feel like a disabled person."

They sat on the first ferry to Bensersiel to pay a visit to the widow of Dieter Wattjes.

"I do not know what you always have ..." Jürgen stirred in his coffee.

"Oh, you know that. I mean, do not you trust me to be able to solve a case on my own? "Eva seemed irritable.

"That has nothing to do with it. And if you remember exactly, it was you who pulled me into the investigation in the Ringmurder case. "

But she had to agree with him.

"But that was only because I'd never managed to call all the registry offices on my own." She looked out of the window and watched the breaking waves. "But it's something else now. I'll ask a widow of a murder victim right now. What should I introduce you to? My chauffeur? "

"Just tell my colleague." Jürgen took a deep breath. Surely this discussion got on his nerves enormously.

Eva did not reply until the ferry docked. And also Jürgen took no new start for a conversation.

"Would you like to have tea with Klara on the way back?" Eva wanted to start the conversation again.

Jürgen shrugged. "If you have time for your exciting job."

"Hey, do not get snapped," Eva grumbled. "I do not mean it. Besides, maybe we could use Klara's car again for the drive to Moormerland. "

"You really understand how to harness people for you," Jürgen snarled.

Clearly one to zero for him, Eva thought. Was it really true that she liked to use other people for her own purposes? She had to think about it when she had time. But that was not the case now. She waved a taxi up and called Klara Bertschoo's address in Esens.

The old lady rejoiced like a snow king over the unexpected visit. She insisted on pampering them with a delicious cup of Ostfriesentee with Wulkje. The tension between Eva and Jürgen evaporated and everything seemed to be in good order again when they got into the old Opel and headed for Moormerland. On the A31 was rebuilt and she was only single lane passable, so that they finally arrived at noon at Sabine Wattjes. As a precaution, Eva had already announced her from Esens so that they could meet her as well. But the way Sabine looked, she would never have left the house in her life. When she fainted the night before, after Mathias Sanders from Leer had delivered the bad news to her, she was in shock and sedation.

"Hello, I'm Eva Sturm," she introduced herself. "And that's Jürgen ... my colleague."

Sabine Wattjes certainly got only half and asked the two into the house. The sunken face was red and eyes swollen. Carefully, as if on ice, she ran ahead into the dining room, where she pointed to a large round wooden table with six chairs.

"Would you like something to drink, maybe a coffee?" Sabine asked in a dull voice. Eva had the impression that she was still under heavy medication.

"No thanks, we just drank tea," she replied. "We're so sorry about her husband."

Sabine Wattjes sobbed and sat down.

"Unfortunately, we have to ask you when you last saw your husband ..."

The widow shook herself and pulled out her handkerchief. It must have hit her hard, Eva thought. Whether children were in the house?

"Take your time," she said. Entering, Eva looked at Jürgen, who held his head on his hand. He looked bored. That was so typical. Could not he feel a little pity?

"It was Friday." Sabine's voice sounded busy. "He was going to Langeoog for this club meeting ... actually, I wanted to go too." She shook herself again.

"And why did not you come with us?" Eva asked.

"Because of this," she said, raising her shaked arm. "I had a bike accident a while ago, so I decided not to ride. But if I had come, maybe ... "She did not finish the sentence and cried again.

Jürgen exhaled audibly. Maybe it's better if he goes out, Eva thought. "Can my colleague take a look around the house?"

Jürgen looked up startled. Was she serious? He should search a strange house?

"Yeah, sure," sighed Sabine. "The study of ... Dieter ... it's straight down the hall and then the first door on the right."

Eva nudged Jürgen under the table and he trotted off.

"Did your husband call you back from Langeoog?" Eva asked.

Sabine shook her head. "No, he has not. But that was not unusual. We've been married for fifteen years. "

Well, if you blunted that way, then Eva was glad that she had been spared so far. What should she ask now? Obviously the Wattjes had been a couple who were no longer interested in each other.

"Did you collect stamps?"

"No, that never interested me. I only went to club events every now and then. «

"Do you know if your husband owns more valuable stamps?"

Sabine nodded. "Of course, there were certainly a few copies here, for which you could get a little money from diehard collectors, that's what Dieter always said. But as I said, I do not know my way around. "

»Yesterday, a swap exchange was planned on Langeoog. Since it would be quite possible that he had taken stamps of more interest on this occasion ... "

"I do not know sorry. But in the study, where her colleague is now, there is also his collection. You're welcome to take everything with you, if that helps. "

Very generous, Eva thought. Maybe a little too much.

"Forgive me if I ask that," she said, "but what was your relationship with your husband?"

"Relationship? What do you mean? "

"Well, you said yourself that they did not talk to each other when he left for a few days. So of course I wonder if they were still very close to each other after fifteen years of marriage. "

Irritated, Sabine looked up.

"There was something ... I think he had another wife."

Aha.

"So you do not know it one hundred percent?"

"Yes, yes. But he never admitted it. It was just a feeling.
"

That women probably afflict more often, Eva thought.

"Did you trust your husband?"

"I've really made an effort ..."

"Was mistrust perhaps the reason why you did not go to Langeoog?"

"No, no way," Sabine said firmly. "Because if I had not trusted him, it would have made more sense to just ride."

Yes, she was right. Where did Jürgen stay?

"I'll see what my colleague does," she said, and disappeared into the hallway.

Sabine ran her hand through her hair. Did she do everything right? She had never been very good at lying before. But the whole situation certainly played into her hands. You would not find out and find out she was on Langeoog.

"What the hell are you doing here for so long?" Eva asked impertinently as she found Jürgen hunched over the desk.

"Now look at this ... meticulously recorded. Each stamp is numbered and listed here with album number and page number. "Fascinated, he gave her the list.

"That's what collectors do," Eva said. "Is it because of what each stamp has a market value among collectors?" Curious she squinted at him.

"And if," said Jürgen triumphantly. "And I'm looking for the stamp with the largest amount in the list."

"The system should be a breeze," Eva said.

"Yes, yes ... I'm about to go." Jürgen kept flipping through. "There," he suddenly exclaimed. There is a gap. The stamp is no longer there. «

"Damn it. What amount are we talking about here? "

"Fifty thousand euros," said Jürgen, his eyes bright. "A lot of wood, if you ask me. It's worth it to give someone a piece of it. "

"Wow ... we have to confiscate the albums. I'll call Mrs Wattjes right away. "

They packed the albums into a large bag Sabine had given them.

"They get everything back," Eva said. "And you really did not know that your husband took this expensive stamp?"

"No, really not. As I said, the subject never interested me."

Eva wondered if the couple had gone so well that they did not need to sell that stamp. And she was even more interested in where and with what money Dieter Wattjes bought this stamp. But it seemed pointless to ask his wife more about it.

"I have a question for Ms. Wattjes," Eva said as she was already standing in the doorway with Jürgen. "Where were you on Sunday afternoon?"

Sabine made a questioning face. "I believe here," she said.

"Unfortunately no," said Eva, "because two officials from Leer have tried to reach you to bring you the sad news. But that did not succeed until they came home late in the evening. Do not you remember calling the police?"

"Of course," Sabine said. Shit, she had not considered that you could have been with her in the afternoon. Had the curious neighbor already chatted about her strange behavior? "I was still with a good friend. We drank coffee and talked, "she said finally.

"Aha. And you drove there with the car? Despite her broken arm? "

So they already knew everything, Sabine thought angrily.

"Yes, it was more bad. It's also the left arm, so I can still switch. "

"But you know that's basically too dangerous and forbidden?" Eva looked serious.

"The blanket just fell on my head."

"What time did you come home?"

Sabine thought for a moment. "Maybe about seven o'clock. But I did not look at the clock. "

"You could have called your husband if you were bored," said Jürgen.

"Well, be that as it may, you have to stay at our disposal should we have any questions. Please do not leave. "

Eva and Jürgen ran to the car.

"Someone's watching us through the window," Jürgen muttered.

"Where?"

"Over there. That must be a neighbor. Shall I ask her again? "

"Stand by," said Eva. She got out of the car and rang the bell at the house.

Jürgen watched as a woman in her fifties opened. Eva talked briefly with her and pointed several times to the Wattjes' house.

"Thanks," she said curtly as she got back into the car. "Your guess was right, this woman has eyes and ears everywhere. And she could tell me when Sabine Wattjes had come home with her car. And it was not at seven o'clock. "She looked wide-eyed as she looked in Jackson's direction.

"So she's lying to us," Jürgen said. "I thought so, that this woman has something to hide."

"Oh yes?"

"Naturally. Show me a woman who does not know how the financial situation is. There's nothing more important to women than the husband's money. "

"You're exaggerating ..."

"And even if she does not care about stamps, I'm sure she knew what treasures there are in the albums. She just needed to look in and google when her husband was at work. "

"Maybe you're right," Eva said. "But first we'll ask the forensics team to see if we can take a look at the stamp albums they've made in the hotel room."

Soon after, the two of them leafed through the albums in the evidence room of the Aurich department. While Jürgen leafed through and looked closely at the stamps, Eva kept the list at hand. Since there were five albums with at least million felt stamps, they decided to spend the night in Esens at Klara. After a short phone call everything was settled. Klara wanted to make potato pancakes for the two for supper. Eva was already running the water in her mouth.

At around four o'clock they had seen stamps from all over the world, but the valuable specimen was not among them.

"I guess the killer took her," Jürgen said conspiratorially.

"Maybe, but then I wonder why he bothered to pick her out of the albums. Why did not he just take everyone along? "

"Maybe the stamp was not in one of these albums," Jürgen guessed. "If that was really so expensive, that Wattjes would have kept it in a safer place."

"But unfortunately not in my safe," complained Eva. "Because then he would surely still be alive."

"You mean he had a date with the killer because he wanted to buy the mark under hand ... and then he just killed him?"

"Brilliant idea," Eva agreed. "That's how it could have been. Now let's go, wait for the potato pancakes. "

People Are Evil

He felt great satisfaction as he put the key in his front door late at night and unlocked it. His hangover, William, ran to meet him. He was a stray and already knew that his master was not there for days. He did not mind as long as there was enough food and he could go hunting at night. Maybe he had that in common with his master.

It smelled musty. In such an old house, it was quickly wet, if you did not ventilate enough. He turned on the lights in the kitchen and ran from room to room, setting the windows down. It was dead quiet outside. Only one bird was sitting in one of the big fruit trees making croaking noises.

William stood beside the kitchen table and mewed. He wanted his reward for keeping the job alone. The man went to the fridge and pulled out a plate of fresh sausage, which he placed on the ground in front of William. The cat ate purring.

The man took his bag with the few belongings and went back into the bedroom. He set it down on the chair with the worn seat and looked helplessly at the large double bed made of dark wood, in which his grandparents had already lain.

He was not tired. He really did not feel anything. William walked in and flipped himself on the colorful self-made coverlet. She had worked on that for four months when she was still alive, the man thought sadly. Whenever he thought of Stella, his heart tightened. She had never done anything to anyone, and yet she died of a nasty tumor a few years ago. It always hit the wrong people. And so that sometimes it hit the right people, you just had to help out sometimes.

Yes. It had hit the right person when Dieter Wattjes had dropped dead on the bed in his room like a wet sack.

So spurred on, the man went back into the kitchen and took a beer from the fridge. He sat down in the old wing chair in front of the window in the living room and looked out into the night.

She

Should she just go back to everyday life? She lolled naked on her silk sheet and played on a long strand of hair. Dieter could write her off now. She felt sad. Yes, very much. And that, even though he had dumped her so easily. Men were like that. And she was used to the fact that these were amicable on their immaculate body, until they plagued the bad conscience. Until they went home to their mum again. Repentant sure none of them felt. And of course they missed the sex with her. But husbands could also go bad if the situation required it. She smiled to herself. She would find a worshiper again, she had no doubt about that. But with Dieter, yes, there could have been more if he could have parted with this woman. She had never understood why that was supposed to be such a big problem. They did not even have children. And now this woman was alone anyway. That could have really helped the jerk.

She laughed, straightened up and took another sip of champagne.

Kartoffelpuffer | Potato Pancakes *(Recipe at the end of the book)*

"The food was really delicious, dear Klara," Eva praised her friend, rubbing her stomach. "But you're removing me from my dream figure by light years."

"I do not know what you always have," Klara said. "You have such a beautiful face. Who's looking at your stomach?"

The two women laughed. Jürgen was just for little King Tiger and got nothing from everything.

"What about the two of you now?" Klara leaned conspiratorially over to Eva. "Have you finally kissed?"

"So Klara, I'm asking you. That's Jürgen, a good friend, nothing else ... "

"You can not fool an old woman like me," Klara chuckled. "I can tell by your eyes that he means a lot to you."

"Oh, right?" Eva pointedly screwed up her eyelids. "And now?"

"Now you have betrayed yourself."

Jürgen came back. Pity, thought Eva. She would have liked to hear from Klara how it was around his eyes.

"Let's play a game," said Klara, who was very fond of this game and rarely had a chance to play it.

Although she was tired, Eva could not refuse her favor. Jürgen agreed to be there.

In the end, Klara had won over four hundred points and Eva gained experience because she saw a mischievous smile in Jürgens face again and again, while his eyes shone. She thought of Klara's words and later fell asleep happily.

The next morning, Eva and Jürgen left very early to take the first ferry to Langeoog.

"What exactly did we find out now," Eva asked, pulling out a sticky note when they sat down at a free table with a cup of coffee.

"That Sabine Wattjes lies like a print," said Jürgen, and Eve noted something.

"And further?"

"Hey, am I with the police or you?"

"I'm training you," she said, laughing. "This is your first intermediate exam."

"Okay, I'll play with you. Furthermore, we know that there is a strong motive with this stamp. «

"If he took her. In principle, we do not know that exactly. We suspect it. "

"Guessing is what's going on in the scene," Jürgen said crookedly. "I can not serve you on the silver platter as a beginner."

"Alright ... keep going."

"It could be interesting to ask if Dieter Wattjes had sex before he was killed ..."

"Yes, that's right. The woman could then be the last to see him alive. "

"And she qualifies as a perpetrator ..."

"Even that. Jealousy is always the strongest murder motive, I do not understand. I would not dream of killing someone out of jealousy. "

"You're different, too."

"What do you mean, different?"

"If a man cares about you, you'll drive him out of the yard before he even marks."

"Pah ... what a stupid saying. I can not help it if men do not meet my standards. "

"Who were there?" Jürgen looked curious.

"Let's leave that now." Eva turned dark red. "We're in the middle of a murder investigation, so go ahead."

The two talked a bit about perpetrators, motives and stamps and ran first to the tourist info when the ferry docked. Anja had everything to Jackson's satisfaction under control. Eva soon said goodbye and ran to the police station. She was curious if the final autopsy report by Ole Meemken had already been received.

She found three messages on her answering machine. One informed her that Heinrich Gerlach had still not been found. Presumably, thanks to the storms of recent days, he had been driven very far to the North Sea. Then somebody from Aurich had called that they needed the safe again if they could spare him. And then there was a call that she could not classify. Someone said in broken German: He lied. Not more. Only these three words. Then it had been reissued. What did that mean? Eva listened to the message at least ten more times, perhaps to recognize the voice. But it was a mystery to her what the caller could have been. And somehow she was sure that it had to be directly related to the murder of Dieter Wattjes.

When she got her computer up, she also found the autopsy report by Ole Meemken in an e-mail. They have not been faxed for a long time. As a result, Dieter Wattjes had drunk and eaten a lot. And that he only had to be dead by a heavy blow to the head as a result of head trauma. And he had had sex. Without a condom, Ole Meemken was sure of that. So he must have known the woman.

Damn, thought Eva. Everything would be so easy if the Wattjes had taken a lover to Langeoog, and then his wife had simply killed him in rage. With her beauty case or whatever. Now, however, they had to think the case over completely. She was already thinking in the plural, she noted with amusement, for she had automatically included Jürgen in the further investigation mentally. Yes, they were both a good team. And he had looked so damned happy playing with Klara Scrabble. She felt that her heart was warm when she thought of him. If only that went well. She quickly ran to the window and let in fresh air.

She had to think back to Heinrich Gerlach, looking at the sea. If she had switched faster that evening, when he had handed her the greasy envelope, then maybe everything would have been different.

The door opened and Jürgen came in.

"There you are," Eva said. »There is exciting news.«

She described in brief sentences the autopsy report.

"At least sex before death," Jürgen said dryly. Eva looked at him questioningly. "Well, surely you treat him as a graduation. And now the motive for jealousy is on the right track. Maybe he was surprised by his wife at the Schäferstündchen and killed with anger. Out of the mouse. "

Eva looked at Jürgen thoughtfully. Most of what he'd just said was probably due to his typically male ego. But there was one thing that was interesting. What if Sabine Wattjes had been on Langeoog?

"And what if she was there?" She said aloud.

"Who was where?"

"Well, the Sabine Wattjes. Just imagine, she was on Langeoog, too. "

"Like right now? She has that broken arm. "

"So what? That did not stop her from visiting her friend. Allegedly anyway. And she might as well have secretly come here to Langeoog to see what her goddess is doing here. "

Jürgen switched slowly. "Understand. But I still do not understand why she turns off the light, because of the little sex ... really unfortunate. "

Eva rolled her eyes. Men were all the same.

"And if she did not want to convict him of stealing, but took the expensive stamp?"

"Ridiculous ... she could have taken her out of the album anytime at home in Moormerland."

"Nice. But who would have suspected Dieter Wattjes first if she had been gone? N / A? Is it ringing? "Eva made circular movements with her fingers beside her temple.

"Then we should ... Pardon, then you should probably check their financial position," Jürgen said pragmatically.

"Exactly." She patted his upper arm approvingly. "And now I have something exciting for you to listen to." She walked to her answering machine and played the last message.

"What's that supposed to mean?" Jürgen asked. "He has lied. That can be all or nothing. It can even be a prank. "

"Is not that a bit far-fetched?" Eva said.

"You have to be there when the kids show up in the pack at the tourist information shop. They have nothing but nonsense in their heads and it goes far beyond our bell pranks of yesteryear. "

Eva went to her desk and sat down. Were you as smart now as you were before? Maybe Jürgen only confused her with his eternal black paintings.

"What is it?" Asked Jürgen, who found it difficult to bear her silence.

"I am thinking."

"Can not you do that aloud?"

"Then I'd have to bully myself ... and you better not say anything now."

In the evening they went to their Italian together, but Eva stayed behind at the Chianti.

The Harvest

The man woke up the next morning at dawn and went into the cold bathroom for a cat wash. Then he cooked water for a nice strong Ostfriesentee. As he sat at the table, he watched William devour his extra dose of cat food. The animal kept looking up at him suspiciously. It was true that animals could not be fooled. They had a sixth sense and surely William knew that this would be their last breakfast together.

When he had packed everything necessary, he climbed into his old Opel captain and left his previous life behind. He left a message on the kitchen table telling William, the black tomcat, to go to a neighboring house one kilometer south if he caught himself. When he looked in the rearview mirror, he had tears in his eyes.

She thought she deserved it. She turned back and forth in front of the big mirror in her dressing room. Did she increase? But what did that matter at the moment, she had her fish on the hook. This old fool actually believed she might go away with him. How stupid did he have to be? If a

97

man thought of the most important piece, it was easy to wrap around his finger.

She had to hurry up, they had arranged to meet at the old barn in Dunum at three o'clock. A Kaff where she had never been before. There he wanted to give her the stamps. And she truly deserved it. Only what she did to the idiot she had not thought about. Her gaze wandered to the cutlery box. Should she take a bread knife? Or better the sharp steak cutlery?

The Body in Dunum

Eva had already pressed the snooze button twice. But now it was time for her to get up. Her head was buzzing with the many discussions with Jürgen. She barely had the opportunity to pursue her own thoughts. But she had to admit that he was not stupid at the search. Anyway, she had to go now.

When she arrived at the police station, the answering machine blinked. The colleague Okko Schuster from Wittmund asked for her recall. It was about the stamp case. Eva immediately dialed the number.

"Hello Okko, you called?"

"Moin Eva. Jo. You've got this case with the club people, and we've just gotten a body that might interest you. "

The colleague made it damn exciting again.

"Indeed?"

"Jo. It is a Wilfried Sievers from Papenburg. He lay in a barn with several puncture wounds in Dunum. Bleed the poor pig. "

"Wilfried Sievers ... that does not mean anything to me at the moment."

"Ne? But that's the chairman of the Stamp Association East Frisia-Papenburg. And I thought that might interest you too. "

Damn, she had not had it on the screen.

"That's a thing," she said. "I'll have to talk to Jürgen right now."

"With whom?" Came the other end.

"Oh no, Okko, can you please send me everything you have about the dead man?"

"That's okay."

"Thank you."

"Jo." Okko hung up.

Eva chose Jürgens number. "You have to come right away," she said. "The club chairman has been killed."

Lurking, she stood in front of the fax machine, waiting for Okko's reports. But she knew that it would take a while for him to move as he spoke.

Another dead man. If one counted Heinrich Gerlach, there were even three, although this was voluntarily divorced from life. But it was a strange accumulation of death among stamp friends. Luckily, she had never been a club person. The door was pushed open and Jürgen came in.

"Another dead man?" He asked breathlessly.

Eva nodded. "My colleague from Wittmund informed me. Wilfried Sievers was stabbed to death in some barn at the end of the world. "

"And where exactly?"

"Dunum, a small village near Esens."

"I'm not coming along so slowly."

"Ask me. We have three dead with Heinrich Gerlach now, within a week. "

"Did you find Gerlach now?"

"Not yet."

"Hm ... what are you going to do now?"

"I'm waiting for the report from Wittmund. And then we have to ... um, I mean, I have to examine the life of Sievers. "

"Do not you want to make a sketch of everyone involved?" Jürgen suggested, pointing to the flipchart.

"A good idea." At the top, Eva wrote the name Dieter Wattjes and branched out to the other names that had been in play so far.

Jürgen had made a coffee in the meantime and now they sat in front of the result and were silent.

"Does that help us now?" Eva asked resignedly.

"I think so," said Jürgen. "Of course you should have put Heinrich Gerlach at the top, because that was the beginning of everything."

"But he was not murdered," Eva countered.

"You can not really know that. The farewell letter may well have been a fake. "

"Do not forget that he handed it over himself. In that sense, I think the letter is genuine. "

"Yes, that's right, of course. But there is not a corpse yet. "

"But he was also a stamp fan. And you have to admit that we have to find the motive there. "

"You also wanted to examine the financial circumstances of Sabine Wattjes ..."

"Yes, I'll do it." Her head was already smoking again. If only at last the stupid report came from Wittmund. Why had she just called Jürgen? She wanted to finally be able to think in peace.

The phone on her desk rang.

"Yes, hello, Langeoog Police Station, Eva Sturm on the phone."

"He has lied."

Then it was launched.

"What is it?" Jürgen asked when he saw Eva's expression.

"That was that anonymous caller again. He lied, he said and hung up. "

"Funny."

Eva ran to the flipchart and wrote to anonymous caller. This branched them with Heinrich Gerlach, Dieter Wattjes and Wilfried Sievers. Because he could have meant all three. One of those men had obviously not told the truth. Whereby she put a question mark in parentheses with Dieter Wattjes, because they had never spoken to him personally. Of course, he could have lied to someone else. It was a damned tricky case.

The fax started and Eva started.

"Finally," she said, pulling out the continuous paper. It did not stop to print.

She scanned the information.

"At least ten knives and fatal ones," she mumbled.

"Wow," said Jürgen. "Someone was mad."

"That's the way to say it. I would almost say it must have been a woman. "

"How come?"

"Experience has shown that men deliberately kill and do not poke around in their victims."

"Well, that's a bit far-fetched, is not it?"

"I do not know, my feeling tells me that a woman must have been damned upset and disappointed with this Sievers."

"Do you think about Sabine Wattjes? Do you think she had a relationship with the Sievers? "

"Would be a possibility. On the other hand, it may have been about the stamps. Maybe she killed her husband, took the stamps, and the chairman got something and blackmailed her. "

"Then why did she kill him in that coffin? How did she lure him there? "

"Women do it, believe me."

"I'm sure," muttered Jürgen. He also jumped when she whistled.

"I think I have to talk to Sabine Wattjes again. Do you want to come along?"

Jürgen thought for a moment, then shook his head. "I think I'll stay here. I can not overuse Anja's good nature either. "

Well, Eva thought, these were new sounds. What was wrong with Jürgen? Had she said, done or thought something wrong?

"Okay," she said. "Then I'll drive alone. It's still early enough for the next ferry. "

Later, when she was looking for a place below deck, Jürgen was already there. Her heart jumped.

"You are here? I thought you did not want to come. "

"I've changed my mind," he said mischievously. "And besides, I assume you'll eat potato pancakes again at Klara's, I did not want to miss that."

After the third ring, Sabine Wattjes finally gave up. Out of the corner of her eye, Eva noticed the neighbor behind the curtain. She would question her afterwards.

"Hello, Mrs. Wattjes, we have a few more questions."

"Come in." Sabine Wattjes looked listless and unkempt. Was that a brutal killer? She went into the dining room, where dishes of the last days piled on the table.

"How are you, Mrs. Wattjes?" Eva asked, looking at the chaos.

The woman shrugged. "How are you supposed to go if you lose the man? I'm left with nothing. "She looked sad.

"We found out that your husband's two albums are missing in the collection," Eva said.

"Oh yes? I did not know that."

"Since your husband listed everything very meticulously in a list, my colleague," she pointed to Jürgen, who looked up in astonishment, "found out. It contained stamps with a collector value of around one hundred thousand euros. And you did not know about it? "

Sabine Wattjes's jaw dropped, making her look even poorer. "I swear, I did not know that my husband bunked such a fortune in his study. We always got on well, my husband had a good job as an engineer. The house here is almost paid off thanks to an inheritance from his parents. The only thing we did not have was children ... "The woman's shoulders trembled as she said that. Eva was sure that she had nothing to do with the death of her husband.

"Was it hard for you ... I mean, you do not have kids?" She asked sympathetically.

"We wanted it that way," Sabine Wattjes said, sobbing. "But it simply did not work out."

"What was it all about? To you or your husband? "

"I do not know that. We were with a thousand doctors. Actually, we could both have ... but somehow we did not harmonize together. "

"You could have adopted a child."

"Yes. Maybe we could have done that. But you know, at some point, the disappointment of your own failure is so great that you have no more strength to look after a strange child. "

"I see." Eva nodded. She really went to the fray of this woman's kidneys. Meanwhile Jürgen apparently counted the tiles of the floor tiles, she said indignantly. "And then at some point in your life there grew the suspicion that he might have a lover, right?"

"Oh, that's not important anymore. Dieter is dead. I do not know what to do next. "

"So it was just a feeling, or was there any concrete evidence, Ms. Wattjes," echoed Eva. After all, she had a murder case to solve.

"Maybe I saw ghosts, but he bought flowers I did not get."

"Did you mention him?"

"No of course not. I found receipts. "

"But they could have been in the company for colleagues or other matters."

"I do not believe that. Some secretary would have done that. No, he sure had another wife, but ... it does not matter now. "She cried. Jürgen let out his breath.

"Good Ms. Wattjes, then we'll say goodbye for today."

As the front door slammed shut, Eva ran straight to the neighbor, who, when she realized they were coming over to her, shamelessly dropped the curtain, which then rocked back and forth.

The woman opened without even having to ring the bell. In the countryside, the walls had ears and slices eyes.

"I thought they'd come back to me someday," the woman said straightaway. "That's too funny with the Wattjes."

"What do you mean by that?"

"Come on." The woman unlocked the door and lured Eva and Jürgen into the house. "Not everyone has to hear everything."

How true, thought Eva, who had the feeling that now many more window curtains were swinging back and forth.

They followed the woman into a lank living room, where green seemed the predominant color.

"What can you tell us about the Wattjes couple now?" Eva began.

"I've known for a long time that something is wrong," the woman said, pushing a cork coaster on the table to and fro. "And now that the Dieter is dead, I'm not surprised anymore."

"What exactly do you mean? What was so strange? "Jürgen asked impatiently.

"When Sabine got on the driveway on Sunday afternoon and did not even get out, I thought she had a heart attack." The woman thumped her chest theatrically. "But then she looked at me ... like a ghost. I asked her if I could help, but she was just scared of it. She almost drove me over my feet. "

"Really?" Eva exclaimed. The whole thing became more and more mysterious, in fact. Then Sabine Wattjes had come home, and because the neighbor had caught her, she had just driven away. By the way, she was with her good friend. The woman lied as printed. And something seemed to make her particularly excited and upset on Sunday. Did she already know that her husband was dead?

"And do you know when Sabine Wattjes returned home?"

The woman thought for a moment and rolled her eyes. "Well, that must have been about nine o'clock. I then gave her the message from the officer from Leer that she should call there. "

"Well, that's it for now, too," said Eva, getting up. "We'll have to go on."

"And I also saw Dieter while he was traveling with another woman," the woman said, as if trying to make things exciting.

"A woman? Where and when?"

"It was not so long ago. I just got off the bike when I saw them on a side street. It was a red sports car. It was a young woman, that's what I saw. "

"And you're sure Dieter Wattjes was in the car?"

"Of course. I saw him walking through my kitchen window shortly thereafter. "

"Did you happen to notice the license plate of the car?" Asked Jürgen.

The woman shook her head. "No, I did not think of it in the excitement. But the car had a big sticker on the back, and there was an advertisement from a law firm on it. "

"Which ones?" Eva asked.

"Meerbusch and Walter, they are in Loga."

"Thanks, that really helped a lot," Eva said.

"I like to help," the woman said with a proud undertone. "You want to know who you're dealing with in the neighborhood."

She brought the two to the door, not without another glance at the house of Sabine throw.

"And now?" Jürgen asked when they were back in the car.

"Well," Eva said. "I'd like to go to Klara's and drink tea now. But I think since we're here on the mainland, we should also visit the widow of the club chairman. "

"Does that have to be?" Jürgen whined. "More gossip?"

"We'll have to talk to her sometime anyway."

"But we already did, when we interviewed everyone at Langeoog."

"That's right, too," Eva agreed. "But her husband was not dead yet."

"She certainly will not say anything else," Jürgen protested. "She probably will not have killed him."

"Do you know?" Eva asked, entering the address of Wilfried Sievers into the sat nav.

However, the questioning did not really lead them any further. Grete Sievers seemed quite composed as they rang the bell at the door in Papenburg. She lived there a beautiful country house right on the canal. There was a lot of land behind the house, part of which belonged to her. Here a lot of money seemed to be involved, because even a large motorhome stood under a carport. And yet, all that did not matter if you were looking for a murder motive.

Then they headed the law firm in Loga to look for the owner of the sports car.

Suspicious and on the flight

"Nice area here," Jürgen said approvingly when they arrived in Loga.

"Yes, people live here with money," Eva said.

The law office was in an old villa with a beautiful bay window. A semicircular wide stone staircase led to the heavy front door, which squeaked tentatively as the handle was pressed down. After a small foyer they stood, as they had gone through the door with colorful ornamental glass, even in front of the reception counter.

Eva introduced them both and came straight to the point.

»We are looking for a lawyer from your law firm who drives a red sports car.«

The young woman with blond ponytail and glasses nodded. "That's Verena ... um, I mean Verena Ferdinand."

"Is Mrs. Ferdinand in the house?"

"Yes, but she has a client right now. But it will not be long. You're welcome to wait in our visitors' room. "She pointed down the hall.

"Is not that all a bit too simple?" Eva asked as she looked through the tall lattice windows into the back garden, which was darkened by a large, old tree population.

"We have not convicted her yet," Jürgen expertly commented. He got routine in the investigative work and Eva wondered if it would soon be time to divide her salary.

"Can I bring you a coffee or water?" The blonde stuck her head inside.

"Water, maybe," Eva said, and Jürgen nodded in agreement.

The employee fulfilled the request and said it would not be long.

"You want to see me?" A tall, slender woman opened the door.

She wore a dark blue costume with a white silk blouse and matching pumps that lasciviously stretched her already slender figure.

At the same moment Eva felt like a sack of flour, when she registered Jürgens not uninterested look.

"You are Mrs. Ferdinand?" Eva asked. The woman nodded.

"We're from Langeoog Police." Pah we. "And we have some questions for you about one, or two, murder victims."

"If I can help, I like to do it. Please come to my office. "

Verena Ferdinand also looked good from behind. Never again potato pancakes and tea with Kluntje and cream.

"Please take a seat." Verena Ferdinand sat down behind her desk and motioned to Eva and Jürgen for two heavy leather chairs. "What is it about? They make me curious. "

The grin will pass you by, thought Eva. And actually she meant both with it.

"It's about the murder of Dieter Wattjes. Does the name mean anything to you? "

The twitching of Verena Ferdinand's mouth had not escaped Eva.

"Yes, I know him," the beauty said, pulling a white cigarette out of a silver case. "They also?"

Eva refused. For both. Out of the corner of her eye she saw that Jürgen grinned like a honey cake horse.

"And how did you know Mr. Wattjes?"

"He was my lover," she said bluntly, giving Jürgen a meaningful look.

"Was he that until his death?" Eva asked.

"No, unfortunately not. He broke up with me a few months ago. Can you imagine that? "Her gaze returned to Jürgen, the little darling jumping out of sight. Well, he could see something when they got back to Langeoog. He could eat his pizza with double cheese, with whom he wanted, but not with Eva Sturm.

"Why did he break up with you?"

"Well, he was married," she sighed. "That's my fate, I always meet men who are already tied."

"And you are not married?"

The woman raised her hands. "No ring, as you can see. I'm still free. "

"That's fine for the male world, I suppose," Eva said shortly. "When did you last see Dieter Wattjes, dead or alive?"

"You have humor, Commissioner," Verena Ferdinand laughed. "It's been a while since I've been with Dieter. And there he was still damn alive. In every relationship."

When Jürgen starts drooling, he flies out, Eva thought.

"And were not you angry that he left her? I mean, it's all about the ego of every woman when a man leaves you. "

"Only if you can not get others," the lawyer countered.

"Where were you yesterday?"

Verena Ferdinand think for a moment. "Well ... so from nine o'clock I was here in the office and had one client at a time ... for consultation."

"I assume your co-worker can confirm that."

"Wait a minute." She pressed long fingers on an intercom. "Miriam, will you come for a moment?"

The door opened the next moment. The ponytail dangled from side to side.

"Mirjam, what did I do yesterday? You're keeping my calendar. "

"Yesterday? You had clients from nine o'clock and I think ... yes, that went on until seven o'clock. That was really a tough day. "

"Yes. Thank you Miriam. "

The door closed again.

So not the Sievers, Eva noted in silence.

"And last weekend? I suppose you will not have worked there, I hope for you. "

"Last weekend? Since I actually had free from Friday evening. And ... yes, now I remember. I visited the cinema with a friend and had a nice weekend. We went shopping and on the piste in Oldenburg in the evening. «

"And this friend surely has a name?"

Verena Ferdinand noted something on a piece of paper. "Here. I wrote down name and address. "

"Thank you. I'd like to have a picture of you, if possible. "

"A photo? What for?"

"For a survey. It just makes things easier if I do not show up with a charcoal drawing. "

Eva imagined how she would put a thick wart right on her nose.

"Well, for my sake." Verena Ferdinand took a picture from a drawer, on which she wore her long hair and smiled at the sun.

"Thank you. That was all ... but wait, I still have a question. Did you know that Dieter Wattjes owned a valuable stamp collection? «

"Stamps?" She spoke as if she were biting a lemon. "No, he did not show me his stamp collection. There was probably no time for that. "She smiled again.

Eva and Jürgen said goodbye, Verena Ferdinand gave him a business card. Eva had seen exactly that. But she said nothing about it, but thought of lonely winter evenings long on Langeoog.

"I do not need to ask you what you think of her," she said straight out when they were back in the car.

"Are you jealous?"

"What? On the long slender legs? I beg you. "She threw the car into the car, put the car in gear, and the transmission yelped.

"Eve, stop it. You really do not need that. "

One more word and I'll kick him out. At the exit she took one of the geraniums. She drove towards Spierkreuzung.

"And now? Are we going to Esenses? "Jürgen grabbed the seat.

"Dunno." At dark orange the journey continued into Bremer Strasse.

"Could you please stop?" Jürgen sounded annoyed. Eva drove right onto the strip for the bus traffic and looked stubbornly out of the side window.

"That bad?" Jürgen asked. "Look, I'm not beauty."

"I know that," grumbled Eva. "That's not what it's all about."

"Rather?"

"Oh, let's just forget it." She turned to him. "I am sorry. That was silly. "

"Just."

"And now?"

"Now let's take a look at the nice yard of Heinrich Gerlach."

"Heinrich Gerlach? How are you coming to this? "

"No idea. But once you're here ... "

"Do you have the address?"

"Jo." Jürgen pulled a crumpled piece of paper out of his jacket pocket. "I bothered to pick out the victims' addresses."

"That's what I call hard investigative work. Where do we have to go? "

"To Ditzumerhammrich," Jürgen read, adding to the street for the navigation system.

"But you know the man lived alone. Who do you want to interview there? He is dead."

"Missing, dear Eva. You're dead when you're dead on the dissecting table. "

Eva was beaten and they drove over the highway through the Emstunnel into the Rheiderland. Just before the Netherlands they left.

"Hare and hedgehogs say good-night," said Jürgen.

"At least." Eva took the narrow winding road across the flat land with the old Opel of Klara, as if leading her to raw eggs.

Then finally they arrived at the single farm of Heinrich Gerlach. Up to the barn it led only a gravel road and to the main house a small sidewalk of paving stones. A half-cleared dung heap had dried up and did not smell anymore. Windows and doors were locked.

"Someone lives here," Eva said. She pressed her nose against a small window and looked through the gap, which revealed a blue and white checkered curtain.

"We have to get in there," Jürgen said pragmatically. "Otherwise the whole exercise was useless."

"Yes. But how?"

"Let me do it." He walked around the house and it took a good five minutes to open the main entrance. The narrow wooden door had peeled off and squeaked as Jürgen pushed down the latch.

"Spooky," said Eva. "I feel like a burglar."

"You are a burglar."

"That someone lives here all alone ... and is also a stamp collector." Eva peered into the small living room with the green upholstered furniture and a small TV set on a black chest of drawers.

Jürgen had run into the kitchen.

"Look Eva, there's something here."

Quickly she was with him. "Do not touch anything," she said as she saw the note on the kitchen table. "What is it?"

"That someone from the neighbors should take care of the black cat. My God, he really thought of everything when he planned to kill himself, "Jürgen said.

"Well, or not," Eva said, glaring at the receipt of a mall that was also on the table.

"What do you think?"

"There." She pointed to the snippet.

"He's been shopping," Jürgen said. He leaned forward. "Among other things, cat food for William."

"Well, but look at the date."

Jürgen read: »Fifteenth of October 2015.«

"Well, is it ringing?"

"Oh man, he was already dead."

"Or maybe not," Eva said triumphantly. "I think the Heinrich Gerlach was a fool."

Updrögt Bohnen | Dried Beans *(Recipe at the end of the book)*

Eva and Jürgen sat with Klara in the living room and clinked glasses.

"The food was excellent again," praised Jürgen. "It's been a damn long time since I ate Updrögt beans."

"Oh, thank you, young man," Klara said. "But it's actually a simple dish. Only today does anyone bother to thread green beans, let them dry and then cook for hours. The young women these days are not learning anymore. "She sighed, letting her gaze wander inside.

"Yes, you are right Klara," Eva agreed. "I've always been too cold to cook. And as good as you, I would not be able to do East Frisian dishes anyway. The sausage and bacon will be remembered on my hips for a long time to come. "

"Oh, Eva, you worry too much about your appearance," Klara said, pouring another grain.

"I always say," Jürgen agreed. "It depends on the inner values. And I'll refine it with a schnapps. "He toasted the women.

They still told stories, with most Klara reported from the past. Eva liked to listen to her. Roads that used to be paths where children used to play in the yellow sand with cars, building roads and castles. Then they had walked through forests, climbed trees, and spent hours watching frogs in ponds. Where was this time? Klara was very sad when she wished the two a good night. Eva went to her and squeezed her again.

"I like your girlfriend," Jürgen said when they were alone.

"Yes, she's a very special woman." Eva's voice had a melancholy sound. "I hope I'm so happy when I'm old."

"You could start with it now." Jürgen poured another glass.

"That's the last one, or I'll start howling."

"I have never understood that women always have to become sentimental when drinking alcohol."

"You do not have to. Let's talk about the case. Since we have done a lot today. And yet we are as smart as before. "

"You just have to sort it out properly. I found the lawyer interesting. "

"I saw that." Eva's mouth tightened.

"I can imagine she has something to do with it. But on the other hand, I wonder why she should need to kill a lover who no longer wants her. She can have ten on every finger. She just needs ... "

"It's good, I got it now," Eva cut him off. "But who murdered Dieter Wattjes? And Wilfried Sievers. How is that related? "

"In any case, stamps are the link to everything." Jürgen had quietly poured himself another and his voice was wider.

"Of course everything is related to that. But I still do not understand why two men have to die for it. And one practically feigns us his death. Have you poured yourself another one? "

"Some things can only be endured in drunkenness." Jürgen giggled thievishly.

"Then I will not be able to expect any great hints from you tonight."

"You can not always think about work, dear Eva." He winked at her.

"And if it's just a stupid coincidence? I mean, it could really be that the two murders happened independently of each other. Unfortunately, they arrived in time so that we think it must be the same killer. Now think about it."

Jürgen cleared his throat and straightened up from his half-lying position in the sofa. "Of course, that could be that the murders have nothing to do with stamps. Or at least one. Sabine Wattjes could have killed her husband out of jealousy."

"You mean, she was on Langeoog, even though she told us something else?"

Jürgen nodded. "Why not. Maybe she finally wanted to catch her husband in red handed and confront him. It is clear that an adulterer would use a trip of several days without his wife to have fun with his lover."

"Well, and then she caught him and killed her with rage instead of talking. That makes sense to me. Would actually make any woman like that. But that she kills Wilfried Sievers is unlikely. She was not tired of them. "

"What?"

"Oh … I meant angrily. I'm already closing my eyes. Do not we prefer to go to sleep. "

"Yes you are right. We're going back tomorrow, right? "

"I do not know yet. But probably. Maybe there was something in the office. "

It was a restless night for both. For Jürgen, because as soon as he closed his eyes, he saw a lawyer lolling lasciviously on her office table. And for Eva, because she simply could not figure out what was actually going on in Jürgen. Why did he run after her like a little dog, if only he had other women in his head? Was it only protective instincts, or did he feel something for them? And if not, what did he want to preserve it for? Again and again she turned in bed, got up again, looked out of the window into the night, where everything was quiet in Esens. She really did feel homesick for her little island. She lacked the sound of the sea right near her. You could really get used to everything and learn to love. Inspired by this thought, Eva eventually fell asleep.

Just when she dreamed of sun, beach and sea, she was rudely awakened by her cell phone. It just rang briefly so an SMS had been received. She looked at the electronic alarm clock. It was just before six. Who in the world? She turned from the bed and walked to the dresser.

I want to make a statement. If you are still in Esens, come over later for a coffee. Sabine Wattjes

What on earth did that mean again? Should she wake Jürgen? But it was still a bit too early for that. So she crawled back into bed and stared at the ceiling. What did Sabine Wattjes have to tell her? Why did she want to talk suddenly, when she had barely spoken before? Something was rotten here. She looked at the alarm again. It was seven at once. So slowly you could really get up. Then she heard how Klara was busy in the kitchen, apparently preparing the breakfast.

Eva ran into the bathroom and jumped into the shower. Maybe the day finally brought the desired solution for all their questions.

"Good morning Klara," she greeted her friend. "That always smells nice when you make coffee. It never smells like that to me. "

"You only think this. But it's always nice to have breakfast elsewhere, I know exactly what you mean. Maybe that's because it's so much more intense. "

She might be right. Who was already in his own kitchen and consciously inhaled the scent when he prepared something? She would try Langeoog, she supposed.

"How long have you been up?"

"Oh, not so long. We talked about the case. "

"Yes, yes." Klara smiled meaningfully. "Want to wake up your partner with that magical smile?"

"Klara, really. There is nothing between Jürgen and me. We are friends, but nothing more. «

"For sure."

Eva went into the hall and knocked on Jürgens door.

"Come on," he shouted. Obviously he was already up.

It almost felt right that she was here with him with Klara. But only almost.

"Sabine Wattjes sent me an SMS early in the morning to say something," Eva said.

"Then you sure want to go back there today, I suppose," said Jürgen.

Eva nodded. "It does not make sense to drive over to the island first. But you're welcome to take the next ferry, I can go to Moormerland on my own. "

"What. I come with. Where I'm in the case. "

Klara peered contentedly at her newspaper.

The Noose Is Closing In

By eleven o'clock, they finally arrived back in Moormerland and rang the bell at Sabine Wattje's front door.

"Come in, I've already expected you."

She made a very disciplined impression on Eva, and the miserable, red-eyed eyes had vanished. Actually, she did not look like Sabine Wattjes, with whom she had felt so much pity on her first visit.

"So you want to make a statement," Eva said. Sabine nodded and asked the two to sit at the dining room table.

"I do not want to hold you long," she began. "It's about this woman my husband had a relationship with. I lied when I said I did not know who it was. "

"So you know her?"

"To know would have said too much. But I know that this is a lawyer working in Loga. Her name is Verena Ferdinand. "

"We already know that," said Jürgen. "We've already talked to her."

Sabine made a startled face that Eva could not yet interpret. "You have not said anything about it yet."

"We do not have to keep you informed of our investigative work, Ms. Wattjes," Eva said firmly. "But it's your duty to tell us everything you know. And now I wonder why you have not said it yet. "

"How do you know it's this lawyer?"

"From your neighbor ..."

"I could have thought so. But I still do not understand how they ... "

"She saw Ms. Ferdinand's car nearby and saw that her husband had dropped out. So she probably put one and one together. "

"Then it certainly knew the whole settlement. How embarrassing."

"Such things are always unappetizing. But how did you know who this woman was? But not from your neighbor? "

Sabine Wattjes swallowed. She still seemed to be close to the whole affair. But Eva felt the whole behavior something set up. What was this woman playing for a game?

"No, it was not the neighbor." Sabine sneered. "They talk about but not with one. No, I saw it with my own eyes when I followed Dieter to Langeoog. "

"You were on Langeoog?" Eva asked, surprised, and Jürgen made a self-satisfied face. He had voiced the suspicion even under the influence of alcohol.

"Yes, I was there. I followed him without him knowing. I just wanted to know if he was meeting another woman there. "

"And? He has?"

Sabine Wattjes nodded. "Yes. It was this Verena Ferdinand. I saw her going to his room in the hotel. It hurt me deeply. I then went to my hotel and immediately drove back to the next ferry. I saw enough. "

"OK. That reminds me, "Eva said," that you first felt the desire to just run away. "

"That would go to any woman like that ..."

"Maybe. But there are also some who then develop enormous anger and do things in affect that they would otherwise never be able to do. "

"You do not think I murdered my husband?"

"It would only be understandable if the backups had blown you," said Jürgen.

"It was not like that. I went to the hotel and then left. I just wanted to go away. If Dieter had come back home, I would have told him that I would get a divorce. Unfortunately, that did not happen anymore. "She gave a tear from the corner of her eye.

Eva did not really believe her feelings. There was something in her eyes that was different from her last conversation. Something had happened to Sabine Wattjes. But what?

"Do you know Mrs. Wattjes, I do not believe you," Eva said. "They told us how much you suffered from your husband's behavior. And then the matter of childlessness. You suspect that your husband is cheating on you, and catch him in the act. And then you want to tell me that you are so in control, that you just go? That's unlikely. "

Sabine Wattjes shrugged and looked coldly in the face.

"I'll tell you what I believe. You saw your accident as a welcome excuse not to go to Langeoog. Then you developed the ice-cold plan to shade your man. And do not tell me that you were not angry when you saw this strange woman go to his hotel room. And then all the emotions, all the injuries of the last years, have come back to you. They felt anger. They hated. This man, because of whom you have renounced everything, she shamelessly deceives. Enjoying a different and, above all, much more attractive woman. Show me a woman who will not lose her nerve. "Eva glanced at Jürgen, who flinched.

"And then you waited until that woman left her husband's hotel room. Agonizing hours in which you imagined what the two are doing. They saw the naked bodies before them, who loved each other in ecstasy. Kissed and stroked. Her husband loved another woman and you could not stand that any longer. Then, when he was finally alone again, they knocked on his door. He was surprised, but he pulled you into the room before you could make a scene. And then he tried to talk to you. Maybe he said that everything is different. That he does not love this woman, that he will stop meeting her. But you, Ms. Wattjes, you were disappointed and hurt to the core. They only felt contempt for him. They did not want to talk anymore. And then you grabbed something, maybe a lamp or a wine bottle and then you hit it. "

Sabine Wattjes hardly showed any emotion. She had listened to Eva calmly. And now she sat there, as if she did not care for the whole thing. As if you have just not been accused of murdering her husband. She seemed uninvolved.

"I can only repeat myself," she finally said. "You're wrong, I did not kill my husband. Why would I have asked you here today for a statement? Would not that have been pretty stupid of me, Commissioner? "

Yes, that would be it, Eva thought. But on the other hand, that might have been part of your plan, you stingy bitch.

"I think you ordered us here today to get us on the wrong track, Mrs. Wattjes. And that's why I'm arresting you with cold bloodshot of your husband, Dieter Wattjes, on account of the urgent suspicion. "

"You make a mistake," Sabine Wattjes said only. "But please, take me with you. Let the real perpetrator get away with it. You have no idea what this Verena Ferdinand is capable of. Believe it, Dieter was the only one who has gone to their games on the glue. There were others. "

"What are you trying to say? Did you observe Mrs. Ferdinand? "Eva asked curiously.

"Yes I have. I followed her for months. Do you think that I am blind? If my neighbor already sees my husband with the slut in the car, why should I have remained unaware? Of course, I've known for a long time that this damned bitch is after my husband. And of course he fell for her. She looks damn good too. Much better than an old wife who has been sitting at the breakfast table day after day for over fifteen years. Of course, you do not have to persuade a man to talk for long. "

Eva squinted at Jürgen. But he wisely stayed behind with approving statements. Luckily she did not get his head cinema with her.

"And you saw Verena Ferdinand with other men as well? Are you trying to say that? "

Sabine nodded. "Yes. There were other men in the game, while she made my husband's eyes beautiful. "

"That would have been the opportunity for you to open your husband's eyes. They could have told him about it, and maybe he would have broken up with her. "

"I really did not want to be naked, Commissioner. First I follow him and then also his lover. In the end, I would have been the hysterical wife again. No thanks."

"You better have suffered for months and then followed them into their love nest on Langeoog, understand."

Sabine Wattjes nodded. "It does not always have to be rationally explainable when it comes to feelings." She cried, and this time, her tears really worked.

"No certainly not. Do you know any of the other gentlemen with whom the lawyer had anything else to do? "Jürgen asked.

"Definitely. It was Wilfried Sievers. "

"The chairman of the stamp club?" Eva asked, astonished. She could imagine a lot, but the verena Ferdinand on the discharge now really not. He was much too old and had a balding bald head. Some of the charms seemed to be slumbering in secret.

"Yes, just that," Sabine said, and blew her nose. "Obviously she did it with half the club."

Maybe that's why the widow of Sievers reacted so indifferently, Eva thought. If she knew that her husband was a stranger, it was quite understandable.

"And you're sure to tell us now that Verena Ferdinand killed Wilfried Sievers, right?"

"Would that be so outlandish?" Sabine said.

"And you certainly already have a motive ready."

"Perhaps Wilfried has heard something about Dieter too ... well, I mean, just imagine, Wilfried's got a lot of hope for Ferdinand. Then he gets along, that also Dieter has something with her. Maybe he just wanted to drink something with my husband and knocked on his door again. And then he gets something from the goings-on of the two. He waits until they are done and Verena Ferdinand comes out. Then he wants to confront the two. But there Dieter is already dead. And the Wilfried is a witness. So she has to get him out of the way, right? "

"That sounds very exciting, Ms. Wattjes. But the question is, why Verena Ferdinand then waited before she killed Wilfried Sievers. Is not that strange?"

"I have no idea. But those are just my thoughts, which I have told you. I've been racking my brains for days on how everything happened. What maybe I could have prevented ..."She sobbed.

"You've seen Verena Ferdinand go to her husband's room. Would not it be conceivable that you could have seen Wilfried Sievers going to see your husband?"

"I said I just ran away. That's the truth. I did not need to know any more than the fact that my husband was cheating on me."

She could be right about everything, Eva thought. And she did not really have anything in her hand to arrest this woman. She even volunteered. But why? That was actually the much more exciting question. Why had she come out with the alleged truth just now?

"Good Ms. Wattjes, we'll finish this at this point. I will not arrest you now, but I urge you not to leave and be at our disposal."

"Of course, Commissioner. I want to help make the terrible story come to an end. "

I believe you even. And I'll also find out why you're in such a hurry now, Eva thought.

"Again to Frau Ferdinand, I suppose." Jürgen had taken the car keys and was walking to the driver's door.

"Yeah, does not it make sense?" Eva was still in thought.

"Then get in."

They lead via the A31 to Leer.

"That did not sound so stupid, what the Wattjes just told us," Jürgen said as they drove through a kilometer-long construction site.

"No certainly not. And maybe everything sounded too good. I mean, we were already with her. But she supposedly knew nothing and lied to us. And then suddenly she remembers a fitting story, where the culprit is served on the silver platter. How does that fit together?"

"That could have been the shock," Jürgen said, threading himself back onto the open lane. "And who does not lie when he realizes he's under suspicion?"

"It can be true that you are right. And yet the whole thing seems too constructed. "

"Maybe because you did not know it yourself."

Why not? Eva wondered. Because the story really sounded too good to be true. A little too nice.

Jürgen stopped in front of the law firm. The red sports car was at the door.

"We have to go back to Mrs. Ferdinand," Eva said to the ponytail, which was worn open today.

"You are lucky," said the young woman. "Frau Ferdinand is free."

She led the two to her office.

"You again?" Verena Ferdinand asked in surprise when she saw Eva and Jürgen.

"We have a few more questions," Eva said.

"Would you like to drink something?"

"No thanks, it will not take long."

The young woman disappeared.

"What else can I do for you?" Verena Ferdinand leaned back, her blouse taut. Jürgen risked a look that Eva registered very well.

"We've just visited your lover's wife, and she said you were a potential culprit." Eva was curious if she would trip over this trap.

Verena Ferdinand looked at her suspiciously. "I'm supposed to have murdered Dieter?" She asked.

"Den, or maybe Wilfried Sievers ... or preferably both. What do you think of this theory? "

"Wilfried whom? The name does not mean anything to me. Who is that?"

"That's the second victim from the stamp club, we told you about it."

"Oh, that. Yes, but I did not remember the name, excuse me. "

"So you did not know Wilfried Sievers personally?"

"It may be that Dieter once talked about him. Maybe I saw him when I was at Langeoog. "

"So, you were on Langeoog, too? You did not tell us that for the last time. "

Such a crap, Verena thought. How could this faux pas happen to her?

Now she had to tell the truth before everything got worse.

"Yes, I lied to you," she admitted. "I went to Langeoog to meet Dieter."

"And then? What happened then?"

"You mean why Dieter is dead? I do not know that. I was in his room after leaving the gala dinner. We had an appointment there ... and, well, you know. "

Jürgen ran his tongue over his mouth. Such a pig, Eva thought.

"Yeah, we can guess what was going on," Eva said harshly. "How did the evening end?"

"Maybe I left about three o'clock. Dieter thought it was better that no one from the club saw me coming out of his room in the morning, that's why. "

"And when you left the room, did not you meet anyone?"

Verena Ferdinand shook her head. "There were people downstairs in the hotel lobby who wanted to go to their rooms. But I did not know her. "

"And you did not meet Wilfried Sievers by any chance?"

"I told you I do not know this man."

"Well, Mrs. Wattjes has testified that you had a relationship with Wilfried Sievers."

"What?" Verena Ferdinand sat back straight and pulled her blazer together. "How does this woman come to it?"

"Because she was watching her for a while, because she knew you had a relationship with her husband. She followed you and saw that you also met Wilfried Sievers. "

The lawyer pressed a button on the intercom.

"Bring me some strong coffee, please," she said.

"And? Is it true now what Sabine Wattjes claims? "Eva asked urgently.

"There was something ... but only briefly," Verena finally admitted to Ferdinand. The coffee was brought.

Yes, all lie here? Eva asked herself. What was wrong with these women? And what happened to her? Why did she lead such a damnably boring life? Maybe she should have something with Jürgen ... that would be a good start.

But now back to the suspects. Should she arrest Verena Ferdinand? Or would you prefer Sabine Wattjes? Her head was buzzing. Or just both? It was quite certain that one of them was the blue of the sky. Who killed who and why? She fervently hoped that not even the widow of Sievers came into play as a perpetrator. And completely silent by Heinrich Gerlach. She also had to take care of the apostate.

But now she first had to solve the puzzle Verena Ferdinand. She had only suspicions. And of course she would have had a motive to kill Dieter Wattjes. If, for example, it had been very different than she pretended to be here. What if Dieter Wattjes had not been so excited about your sudden appearance in his hotel room? Had not he dumped her for the sake of his peace with his wife? That could gnaw at the ego of such a vamp, even if she could still have so many men. What if she had wanted only this one?

"Admit it," said Eva suddenly, "you loved Dieter Wattjes. I mean right and not just as a pastime, as it seems to be so usual. And then you could not bear that he left her because of his wife. A woman he does not love anymore. They wanted him to love you and only you. But he was not ready for that. He managed to break up with you. Men can do something like that. But it was different with you. It gnawed at you like a sharp sting. They wanted him back with skin and hair. They followed him to Langeoog without his knowledge because you thought you could get him back then. But that did not work out then. They knocked on his door and he was not thrilled to see you. Of course he would have done nothing better at this moment than to go to bed with you. But he knew everything would start all over again. So he rejected her with a heavy heart. And you, who just wanted to give him your true love, you have been incredibly disappointed and angry. So angry that you grabbed something and slammed it. Maybe you did not want to kill Dieter Wattjes, but then he suddenly lay there on his bed in all the blood. And out of sheer panic, you ran out of the room. You probably ran into Wilfried Sievers on the way. He may have wondered to meet you there. But he probably did not switch until he found his club mates dead. "

"You've gone completely crazy." Verena Ferdinand had jumped up. "That's an absurd story you'd like to point out to me here."

"You can take a lawyer," said Jürgen.

"Very funny," she replied venomously.

"When did you decide to kill Wilfried Sievers, too?" Eva interjected. "Did he maybe blackmail you?"

"What was he going to blackmail me with?" The lawyer asked contemptuously, then sat down again. "That old fool was too stupid for that."

"Well, I'm not so sure. It could be that he wanted to force you to start something with him again. He would then shut up. And since you did not want that, you lured him into an ambush in the barn in Dunum and stabbed him in cold blood. "

"You figured something out, Commissioner. But do you have the slightest proof of your insinuations? "Verena Ferdinand seemed completely composed again.

Somehow I missed the moment when she would have blabbed everything out, Eva thought. Now she was completely buttoned up and in control. And she was right.

There was not the slightest proof. They were missing in both cases, the murder weapons. She had admitted that she had been in the hotel room. But what good did it do?

"May I look around your apartment, Ms. Ferdinand?" Eva asked.

The recipient answered with a smile and nodded. "Do not force yourself, I have nothing to hide."

That I'm not laughing, Eva thought.

They drove after Verena Ferdinand, who willingly took her to her apartment. Everything was bright and modern. Just as you always saw in these many lawyer series. She sat relaxed in the living room and watched the investigator as she inspected one room after another. Eva had asked Jürgen on flimsy grounds to drive once more to Leer's local office. She did not want her hobby investigator to snoop around this clever woman. If they found out who Jürgen really was, then it was over for them and the beautiful days on Langeoog.

There was not much that Eva noticed in this apartment. Obviously, Verena Ferdinand had a thing for Swarovski crystal figures glittering in a glass cabinet. Then a bookshelf with literature and the one or the other romance novel. In her bedroom, furnished with white furniture in real wood, she found a vibrator in the bedside drawer. Obviously this woman could not get enough. In another drape were neatly sorted panties and brassiere made of silk and other frivolous materials. What had she expected? That here a crowbar and a butcher's knife were just waiting for her, so that she could convict this woman. And then she found under satin sheets still a cloth bag. When she raised him, he was heavier than she had thought because she had suspected socks or the like in it. But when she pulled the drawstring on, she said coins. Pennies from D-Mark times. Two and one. Funny, that did not suit this chic woman at all. Was that about money for bridal shoes? Something like that was done earlier. But Verena Ferdinand was far too young for that. That made no sense.

"You have a really nice apartment," Eva said as she returned to her suspect's room. "

"Thank you, I appreciate her praise," Verena Ferdinand said supremely. "Did you find something? Was it all worth it for you? "

Eva thought of the vibrator.

"You collected coins?" Eva asked.

"Coins? What do you mean?"

"I found pennies in your laundry," Eva said, looking forward to the twitching of Verena Ferdinand's eyes.

"Oh, that?" Verena Ferdinand said quickly. "That's from my mother. She collected money for bridal shoes for me when I was a little girl. "

"But you have not used it so far," said Eva. Somehow, her counterpart had a sad expression.

"No," Verena Ferdinand laughed. "And in the meantime, I would have to spend euros on that."

"If you meet the right person," Eva said.

The lawyer nodded and looked out of the window as if she saw something there, which was hidden from Eva.

"With Dieter Wattjes, it could have been something, am I right?" She asked in the resulting silence.

"I loved him," Verena Ferdinand said in a husky voice. "I really loved him." Then tears began to stream down her face, letting the fine skin shine in the falling sun.

"Now tell me what really happened on the night in question when Dieter Wattjes died."

Verena Ferdinand got up and ran to a small display case, from which she took a noble-looking bottle of amber-colored contents.

"One too?" She asked, and Eva nodded. After all, she had a driver with her.

The lawyer came back with two swivels and put one in front of Eva before she sat down again.

"It was like I said, I went to Langeoog because I wanted to be alone with Dieter again."

"How did you know he was going alone?"

"I took care of it."

"As?"

"His wife, the accident. I hit her. "

Eva jumped in shock. She would not have thought that now.

"That sounds brutal to you, but I did not see any other way. Dieter had refused to meet again in Leer or Moormerland or elsewhere in East Frisia, because he assumed that his wife suspected something. Maybe he even

154

knew she was spying on him. In any case, he did not want that anymore. And when the excursion came, I thought I might be able to help fate. "

"You could have killed Mrs. Wattjes," Eva said indignantly. "Was that really worth it?"

"Have you never loved, Commissioner? And she survived it. "

"Probably true. But not her husband. Tell me more. «

"Dieter agreed to meet me on Langeoog when I sent him a text message. But it could not come out under any circumstances, that was his condition. So we made an appointment to go to his room the night after the gala dinner, when most of them would get drunk anyway. "

"What happened there?"

"We loved each other. It was so nice. And it was also unique for Dieter, that's exactly what I felt. A woman feels that, does not she? "

Eva was really over-excited. She had to catch up a lot.

"And? Could you persuade Dieter Wattjes to get back in with you? "

Eva already guessed the answer.

"No. After having had his fun, he explained that this would be a one-time thing. When we got home, he did not want to see me anymore. He was so mean. I cried, implored him. I told him I could not live without him ... but he, he just kicked me out when it got too much for him. "

The tears on Verena Ferdinand's face had dried. The shine was gone. Also from her eyes.

"Did you kill Dieter Wattjes, Frau Ferdinand?" Eva looked at the accused. Yes, she almost felt sorry for her.

Verena Ferdinand said nothing, she only nodded.

"How?" Eva swallowed.

"I got dressed again and headed for the door. For Dieter, the matter was well done with it. But there was a seething in me. I was hurt and felt used and dirty. When he went back to bed, thinking it was finally quiet, I went back and told him ... I ... "She shook herself.

"What do you have?"

"I've got the purse over his head ..." She groaned. "It was such a terrible sound. It cracked. Dieter immediately fell forward. He did not move anymore. But I did not want that at all. He should only feel something of my injuries, you understand? "

"You mean the pennies? You killed Dieter Wattjes with her bridal shoe money? "

Verena Ferdinand nodded again. "Yes. I took it with me because I wanted to show Dieter how serious I am with him. I wanted to surprise him. "

"You succeeded, too," Eva said dully. What a frightening end to a great love, she thought. Maybe she should rethink her planned activities with Jürgen yet again.

"I have to arrest you, Ms. Ferdinand," she said.

"All right ..." The lawyer rubbed her face.

"What about Wilfried Sievers?"

Verena Ferdinand shook her head violently.

"No, I do not have that on my conscience. You have to believe me. I did not even see him on Langeoog. He could not have known that I was in the room with Dieter. "

Eva wondered why she should still lie now. She had already confessed to a murder. There it would not have arrived on another one. So she probably said the truth. But who stabbed Dunum? In her germinated a suspicion that was only vague and yet tangible.

She called her colleagues at the office in Leer to send a car to take Verena Ferdinand to Aurich.

Back on Langeoog

Jürgen had insisted that they return to the island on the same day. He was a little miserable because he had not gone to Verena Ferdinand's apartment. But he already understood Eve's reasons. For compensation, she invited him in the evening to her favorite Italian. Double cheese always helped in such difficult situations.

"That was a successful day," said Jürgen and smacked.

"Yes," Eva agreed, drinking from her Chianti.

"But you're not looking really happy."

"I have another surplus corpse, do not forget that. I do not need a suitable murderer. "

"Or murderess," Juergen said.

"But I believe Verena Ferdinand that she did not kill Sievers."

"That's okay. You have one more candidate. "

"You do not mean Sabine Wattjes. Why in the world would she have killed the Sievers? "

"No idea. But finally she has rushed you to the trail of Verena. And with announcement. She's insisted on testifying, remember?"

"No, of course not," said Eva gruffly. But that also always Jürgen brought the strings together.

"You see," said Jürgen triumphantly, "if you did not have me." She thought about the vibrator again. Hopefully, she soon got him out of her head again.

"You're right, I thought about it," she lied shamelessly. "But what motive should Sabine Wattjes have for killing Wilfried Sievers?"

Jürgen snipped his pizza further apart and pushed himself piece by piece with relish in the mouth.

"That's a very exciting question," he said, tipping down the first Massala. "In that case, it could have been Dieter."

"How do you mean?"

"Well, if this Ferdinand had something to do with the Sievers, too, if only briefly, then yes, Sabine Wattjes ... oh, I do not know. Somehow I'm just talking nonsense right now."

As so often, Eva thought.

"Yeah, it seems to be the wrong approach, too," she said aloud. "But what if it was really about stamps, not sex?"

"How boring," said Jürgen, laughing.

"Just think ... or at least try it. The valuable stamps of Dieter Wattjes are still missing. "

"You mean, the Sievers ...?"

"Maybe. Because it could be that Sievers knew that Dieter Wattjes wanted to take some to Langeoog. But he told us that he knew practically nothing. "

"And then somebody called you and said he lied."

Even Eva fell again the call again.

"That's right, someone said he lied. That could mean Sievers. "

"Well, if only we knew who called."

"And if it was Sabine Wattjes ...?"

"But the voice sounded rather ... well, I do not think so. It did not sound like someone from here. "

"That's all wrong. Maybe she wanted to confuse us from the start. "

"But why? She did not kill her husband. "

"No not that. But she may have used the opportunity cleverly and brought the stamps to her. "

"But that does not make sense if the Sievers got their hands on those things."

"Oh, maybe. Because if Sabine Wattjes was not so unaware as to her husband's collection, then it was easy for her to get in contact with the chairman and talk about the loss. "

"Hm ... and he felt caught because he took the stamps when he found Dieter Wattjes dead, so he confessed everything to her."

"Bingo. And she blackmailed him. Maybe she even wanted to share with him. Or not. But she lured him to Dunum, I'm pretty sure of that now. "

"That would be a joke, if the Wattjes were the Sievers ... really." Juergen looked at his knife and imagined her ramming something similar. Women could be so brutal.

"Now we just have to prove it to her," Eva said conspiratorially. "I think we have to go to Moormerland again."

"I was afraid of that," sighed Jürgen. "When do we leave?"

"Tomorrow with the first ferry," she said mischievously.

Murderer

She washed her face thoroughly and rinsed with cold water. So slowly, the swelling of the eyes went back. Finally. She looked so ugly with her red-rimmed eyes, she found. But at least they had taken her from her, that she was devastated. And now she had to bring order to her life. No longer feel the monotony of everyday life. No longer overly curious neighbors endure whom she would have preferred to have turned her neck. Never would she have dreamed that she was capable of such aggressive feelings. But her husband had taught her better. Why did he have to do something with other women? Only because she could not have children? It was not her fault if the two of them did not work. Could not one be happy, without? She had tried. But he had become more and more involved in this stupid hobby. Ironically stamps. If he had at least become a motorboat driver. Then you could have gone out together and met nice people. From time to time drive to a small East Frisian island. Many did. But he had not been interested when she had put a promotional leaflet on the table. Water was not for him, he had meant and thrown the thing in the trash. Instead, he had dragged her along to those unspeakable humans, who talked shopliftily over paper bits all day long. And she could not talk to the women either. The most stupid as bean straw. Only the man, his food and the gossip of the neighbors on the subject. What should she do with them? She would be almost desperate for it.

She tried to find a job to change her mind. But in her mid-thirties, she was too young for some, as she could still have children and the other already too old, because they lacked important PC skills. Her self-esteem had plummeted further and further into the basement.

And then Dieter started to collect women as well. Just when she was feeling so bad, she had found the first receipts. Was she really surprised? Were not all men alien? Maybe. But she just did not want to let that happen. Did not want to bother with the constant thought of who he was holding in his arms and caressing.

She could not say today when the devilish plan came. But at some point she got into conversation with the chairman. He had first told her what her husband, Dieter, was doing for an interesting and lucrative hobby. His collection is already worth a lot. And that was not out of Sabine's mind. She had made herself nauseous. Researched the internet, ordered collector books and listed everything exactly. And in the end, she knew there was a small fortune in her house she had not known before. And now she was all alone. All she had to do now was finish everything.

She was just starting to pack her second suitcase when the doorbell rang. Who could that be at this time? She did not expect anyone. And it did not suit her either. Undecided, she went to the door and stopped shortly before. She did not have to open.

It was rung again. Obviously, it was a stubborn person. Before her curious neighbor took matters into her own hands, Sabine opened up.

"Good morning Mrs. Wattjes. I hope we do not get it wrong? "Eva noticed that the woman in front of her was not exactly out of bed or under the shower. So why had it taken so long for her to open?

"You? Is there something else? I do not really have time. "Sabine smoothed her fingers through her hair.

"It does not take long. Just a few more routine questions. "Eva put the first foot into the house. "Do you want to go away?"

"What? Me no."

"I just thought, because I see a travel bag there. Policemen do not miss anything, unfortunately. "

"Oh, that's right. Yes, it's true. I wanted to change my mind. "

"But we asked her not to go away."

"I thought after the last conversation that everything was so clear. You arrested the lawyer, right? Anyway, that's what my neighbor told me. "

"Yes, dear neighbors. That's right, we arrested Verena Ferdinand. And she even confessed to killing her husband. "

A short smile flickered over Sabine's face.

"I told you so ... what can I do for you now?" She headed more relaxedly forward into the dining room. "Am I supposed to make a coffee?"

"We thought you were in a hurry. But yes, gladly. "Eva did not take her eyes off her. Did she think she was safe now? In any case, her movements were safer.

Jürgen threw a glance into the study of Dieter Wattjes before he followed him into the kitchen. A feeling told him something was wrong. Carefully, he opened the door.

"What are you doing?" He suddenly heard Sabine Wattjes behind him.

"A routine check," Jürgen replied. "Do you have a problem with it?"

"You've been snooping around. But do not force yourself. "She turned on her heel and headed back to Eva's kitchen.

"My colleague can not help it," Eva said apologetically. "Sometimes he just looks for the famous needle in a haystack."

Sabine poured coffee and sat down next to Eva.

"I'm so glad it's all over."

"Yes, I believe you. It is certainly a great relief to know that your husband's murderer has now been arrested. "

Sabine nodded.

"What will you do now?"

Sabine shrugged.

"I'm not entirely sure. Maybe just get out and then clear your head. You know, such a long marriage, even though admittedly there were difficulties, you do not shake off so easily. I loved my husband. "She put a painful undertone into her voice that Eva did not buy from her.

"Does not it matter to you whether Verena Ferdinand confessed to the murder of Wilfried Sievers?"

"Certainly ... but that's what I was going for."

"See, and that's the difference between you and us investigators. We always want to know exactly. We do not rely on our feeling. That's why we came back here today. "

"I do not understand ..."

Jürgen came into the kitchen and nodded to Eva.

"Did you find anything else?"

"Yes," said Jürgen. "But it was not easy."

Sabine looked disturbed from one to the other.

"What did you find? What does all this mean? "She shifted her coffee cup on the table top, uncertain.

"I've found a laptop that's yours," Jürgen said matter-of-factly.

"A laptop?" Eva repeated, interested. "Where, then?"

"Between the underwear of Mrs. Wattjes?"

"They were in my bedroom," Sabine screamed. "What were you doing there? I did not allow you that. I want to see the search warrant immediately, otherwise ... "

"Anything else, Mrs. Wattjes?" Eva stared into her face. She saw in it only contempt. "What was on the laptop?" She asked Juergen.

"Exactly what we suspected," said Jürgen. »Lots of information about stamps. And that, though Mrs. Wattjes is not really interested in it. "

"Allegedly ..."

"I agree. And then there were the lists we found in Dieter Wattje's study. "

"Interesting," Eva said. "But I'll bet we will not find a fingerprint of him on it. Right, Mrs. Wattjes? "

"I do not know what you're suggesting to me. I want to see my lawyer right away. "

"Oh, you'll need it, too," Eva went on. "Because you've been wondering what your husband's stamp collection was worth. He did not care so much about it, he just loved his hobby."

"You're crazy," Sabine exclaimed. "This will have consequences."

"I'm sure," Eva said quietly. "And Jürgen, did you find the missing albums?"

"I'm still here. Now I'll get to know the suitcases of Mrs. Wattjes."

"Yes, do that. And now back to you," she said to Sabine. "Do not you want to finally tell me what connected you to Wilfried Sievers? Did you incite him to steal the albums your husband took on the island?"

Sabine's eyes flickered. Eva almost had the impression that she was about to faint. But she held on to the table and took a deep breath.

"What would you have done in my place?" She suddenly asked in a low voice.

"An unhappy marriage does not excuse everything, Mrs. Wattjes," Eva said. "When did you make the terrible plan of getting your husband back?"

"It was all just pure coincidence," Sabine began to tell. "It all started when I did not trust my husband anymore. Everywhere I saw ghosts. Any woman he looked at for more than three seconds was a danger to us ... to me. It was a vicious circle that I could not get out of at some point. I searched everything. Can you imagine what that feels like when you turn your husband's things upside down every day? "

She poured herself another cup of coffee. Eva refused.

"And at some point I even searched the stamp albums. What I hoped to find there, I do not know. But I've dealt with it, I've got books on it. I was obsessed. And then I discovered how much money was behind it. I had never been so aware. And honestly, I do not know how Dieter financed it at all. Obviously he duped me in every way, you know ... "She looked sad, for the first time Eve saw the pain of a desperate woman flashing. She had to go through a lot.

"How long has it been that you meticulously recorded everything?" Eva asked.

"Maybe a year," Sabine replied.

"And when he kept cheating on you, did you decide to pay him back?"

"I do not know. That was not so concrete. When the trip to Langeoog was due, the accident came to my heart. I decided to use my injuries as an excuse that I could not ride. And then I decided to pursue him secretly. I just wanted to see what he was doing. "

"And how did Wilfried Sievers come into play?"

"Oh, that's a stupid story. When I watched the hotel from the outside, he ran into my arms with a stupid mishap. I was hiding behind a hedge and he had to go, if you understand. "

Eva nodded in confirmation.

"He was very drunk and laughed stupidly when he recognized me. In his drunkenness he would have done the most stupid things, but I wanted to remain undetected. So I persuaded him to shut up. "

"As?"

"Oh, you do not want to know that. In any case, it was uncomfortable. But I was successful. When he was sober again, I just told him everything. And he told me about the valuable stamps Dieter had taken to Langeoog. He wanted to present her proudly at the exchange, Wilfried told me. And besides, Wilfried planned to propose Dieter as the new chairman. It should be a great day for Dieter. "

Well, that went awry, Eva thought.

"What happened next?" She asked.

"I told Wilfried that my husband was cheating on me. And that I could not take it anymore. He had a lot of understanding for me. I had always liked it, I knew that. So I persuaded him to help me. He was supposed to steal the stamps from Dieter's hotel room and we would share the loot. "

"And Herr Sievers agreed to that?"

Sabine nodded. "I did not need to persuade him long, if you understand. He sneaked into the hotel when it was already very late and everything was quiet. He just wanted to get the stamps and then he discovered Dieter lying dead on the bed. "

"And he did not call the police right away," Eva said, "but he stole his dead friend and just left him there."

Sabine nodded. "Yes, he did. We were both shocked that Dieter had been killed, believe me. But what else would have changed if we had called the police? And the stamps are mine, after all. Either way."

"Who took the stamps? Was that Herr Sievers?"

"Yes. We decided because Dieter was dead. It was clear that they would come to my house. It would have been better if they had not been there."

"You mean, because then you would have figured you might have stolen the stamps from the hotel room? How could the police have known they were there at all?"

"You never know. Maybe Dieter had entrusted himself to someone from the club. And then you would look for the stamps, that was our idea."

"I see," Eva said. There was a lot of criminal potential in this woman. "And you phoned me at the police station, right?"

Sabine nodded. "It was just a distraction maneuver. We thought you were busy for a while."

In fact, Eva thought. Quite torn.

"When did you decide that you would rather have the whole loot for yourself?"

"Oh ... somehow I did not really care about Wilfried. Besides, why should I give him any of my property? "

"They had a deal with him."

"Yes. But when I got home, things looked very different again. We had arranged to meet in the barn in Dunum, a small town where no one can go and where nobody knows us. "

"You took a knife? Did you already plan to kill him? "

Sabine shook her head violently. "No, definitely not. I just wanted to scare him. He should see what I could be capable of. But then the whole thing escalated. He called me a bitch. I should keep my word. He was not ready to give me the whole collection, so I had to do something ... "

"You stabbed him, more than once."

"Yes."

Jürgen came back into kitchen. Eva thaught, he was listening behind.

»Here they are«, he sad and shows two books held in his hands.

Eva calls the other detectives in Leer and told them, that there is an another murder too, that should be taken to Aurich.

Ditzumerhammrich

Eva and Jürgen went to the office in Leer, because Eva wanted to personally thank the colleagues for the good cooperation. She met Commissioner Guntram, whom she first saw in person. She was impressed with him because she had heard a lot about his cases.

"I hope you left some gangsters for me," joked Guntram.

"Of course," laughed Eva. "It was just coincidence that the two murderers came from your territory."

"A new colleague?" Guntram asked, pointing to Jürgen.

"Oh ... no," Eva avoided, before Jürgen said something wrong. "That is coincidence."

Guntram raised his eyebrows but did not ask.

"Do you want another coffee?"

"Oh, no thanks," Eva said. "We did not want to stay long."

"Well, too bad my two colleagues are not here right now. Mathias and Katrin would have liked to meet you once. "

"Something's going to happen again," Eva said. "Now we want to go to Ditzumerhammrich."

"What are you doing there?" Guntram asked, and Jürgen looked surprised too.

"There's an unexplained case that's also related to the stamp collectors."

Eva briefly described what happened to Heinrich Gerlach. And that they suspected that he could have done something wrong.

"I do not know this name," Guntram said. "I'm sorry. But if I hear something, I'd like to let you know. "

"That would be nice," Eva said. "So, and now we have to go on."

"What's that supposed to mean?" Jürgen asked as they sat in the car again.

"I did not want to stay there longer than necessary," Eva said. "And besides ... why should not we go to Ditzumerhammrich again? Maybe Heinrich Gerlach has reappeared and we are unnecessarily worried. "

"I do not believe that," said Jürgen. "But in the name of God, let's go to the end of the world."

The farm looked as deserted as it had on their last visit. Even the door was still open.

"Has the cat been taken care of?" Eva asked.

"Shall we go in?"

Eva nodded and they got out.

When they came into the house, it smelled musty. The heating, if there was one, did not work. And the individual wood-burning stoves smelled of stale ashes. Nobody had been here.

"William!" Exclaimed Eva, hoping the animal would answer. But it remained silent.

She ran to every room where she faced loneliness. What had Heinrich Gerlach led here to a hermit existence? Did anyone even miss him besides his pet?

"Who are you?" Eva suddenly heard a young female voice say. She turned around. Behind her stood a young woman who looked at her in astonishment.

"My name is Eva Sturm, I'm a policewoman. And who are you?"

"I'm Wiebke Gerlach. This is my grandfather's house. "

"Oh. And do you know where your grandfather is? "

The young woman shook her head regretfully. "No, unfortunately I do not know that. I live further away and visit him here once in a while. He does not have a phone, so I can not call him first. "

"Understand. And his cat? Have you seen them? "

Wiebke Gerlach shrugged. "No," she said. "But what are you doing here? Has anything happened to my grandfather? "

"We do not know that exactly. That's a longer story ... "

Eva told Wiebke about the incident on Langeoog and that they suspect that her grandfather had to be here again.

"That's all weird," said Wiebke. "It does not go with Grandpa to let his cat down."

"Maybe he was lonely," Eva said.

"You mean he's done something wrong?" Wiebke asked, startled, tears gathering in her eyes.

"Are you the only one who visits him here?" Eva asked.

Wiebke nodded. "I think so. Grandpa does not have many friends. Most of them are already dead. And he does not like people, he used to say that. "

Eva understood that in a way. Where had Jürgen actually gone? It was worse with him than with little children. Surely he was just turning the whole farm upside down.

"But her grandfather liked animals ... and he liked her," Eva said comfortingly. "I'm sure he has a better life where he is now."

"But he can not just leave me alone," sobbed Wiebke and began to cry.

Eva took the young woman in her arms and tried to comfort her.

But there were things that just took their time.

When Wiebke had calmed down a little, they walked together through the house and the young woman spoke with shining eyes of the many hours she had spent here. Of the many stories her grandfather had told her from before, from another time, when the world was still in order. And eventually even William came crawling out of a corner and lolled sleepily.

"You see," Eva said. "We've already found the first outlier."

"He just slept, the old slacker." Wiebke laughed again and picked up the animal. "Grandpa loves you very much, William. He'll be back soon. "

But Heinrich Gerlach would not appear again in Ditzumerhammrich, but they could not know that yet.

Eva and Wiebke found something in the house that he had placed there expressly for Wiebke.

"A stamp album?" Wiebke asked in surprise. "What am I supposed to do with it?"

"Your grandfather would have thought something of it," Eva said. "Maybe they are worth a small fortune. I, if I were you, would have it checked. "

Wiebke made a sad face. "The way you say that, it sounds like my grandfather would never come back." She swallowed.

"That could be, Wiebke. But nobody can know that until you find him. "

"I'll stay here in the yard," said Wiebke firmly. "It has always been my dream to build a small farm. Maybe Grandpa wanted to give me a sign with that one. "She pointed to the album.

"And what will your parents say about that?" Eva asked.

"Oh that. You've always said that I'm just as vile as Grandpa Heinrich. You will not be surprised. "Wiebke could laugh again.

"Well, I think, my colleague and I, we'll have to go back. Can we leave you alone here? "

"I'm not alone," said Wiebke. "William's with me. And I'm sure Grandpa will see me no matter where he is right now. "

Eva looked into the rearview mirror until the court of Heinrich Gerlach had become a very small point.

"Eva, you worry too much," said Jürgen, noticing she was about to cry.

"Leave ..." Eva said. Then she blew her nose. She was glad that Jürgen drove, she could hardly see the road through the thick veil of tears.

Only when Klara arrived in Esens to return the car did she regain her grip.

"It was so nice you two were here," Klara said again and again.

"Yes, we really enjoyed the good food," Jürgen said.

"Come back, young man." Klara winked. "Next time I'll make fresh kale for you with cabbage sausage and mettenders."

"I can not wait." Jürgen's mouth watered.

"You spoil him too much," Eva said, laughing. "On the island he mostly eats pizza with double cheese."

"But that's not healthy," Klara said. "Is no one cooking any more these days?" She looked pensively after them as they climbed into a cab to drive to the ferry dock.

On the ferry, Eva rummaged for her cell phone and called her colleague Okko Schuster in Wittmund.

"The murder of Wilfried Sievers is cleared up," she said against the wind.

"Really now?" Okko shouted into the phone. "Class."

"Yes. The murderess is sitting in Aurich. And my case on Langeoog is solved. Now we're going back to the island. "

"Why do you always say we always? Who is this man you are traveling with? "Okko Schuster asked, who had been approached by other colleagues several times before that they only saw Eva in company.

"Oh, that's coincidence. A good friend who has a car. That makes me more mobile on the mainland. "

"Ah," said Okko Schuster. "But you could have a company car from us, you know that."

"Yes, yes ... but that's fine." If you knew, she thought, and laughed to herself. But it was really better if they made the further cooperation a bit more discreet. It's hard to imagine what kind of trouble she would get if it came out that Jürgen now conducted regular surveys and searches. Somehow the whole thing had gotten out of hand.

She ended the conversation with Okko Schuster.

"Well, what does your colleague say? Were we good or were we good? "Jürgen had half listened.

"Oh, just stop. It is probably already rum around that I have a shadow. We should be more careful. "

Jürgen registered very well that she was interested in further cooperation with him. And that made him happy. He also enjoyed it. Not to imagine if he should return to his little exciting life exclusively in the tourist information. No, it had been exactly the right moment for Eva to come to the island.

"Pizza tonight?" He asked, laughing.

"Always happy," Eva said.

Island Breeze

Several weeks had passed and Eva had re-established herself in her little life on the island. She was looking forward to the winter. Then not many people would be on Langeoog. And hopefully no clubs, she thought as she looked out the window of her small office at the dunes. In the sky thick clouds pushed on a long journey. Eva felt well. She would never have believed that when she was moved here a year ago. And also with Jürgen it was always better. They were a well-rehearsed team. Everyone knew where the frontier was, which was better not crossed. He had asked her if they did not want to celebrate Christmas together. Yes, why not? She had said.

THE END

Dear reader. I hope you enjoyed the thriller. I would now like to point out the continuation, which was published in December 2015. Then there's a Christmas thriller with Eva Sturm on Langeoog, where Heinrich Gerlach will mysteriously come across you again.

Recipes

If you fancy a potato pancake and some extra beans, then here are the recipes for you:

Potato pancakes, as I like them, according to a recipe of my grandmother from the former East Prussia

Ingredients for 2 - 3 people

2 kg of potatoes

3 larger onions

4 eggs

Salt pepper

Preparation: You rub the onions and the potatoes with a machine (in the past I learned this with difficulty with a hand grater with Granny). Then add the whole eggs and season with salt and pepper.

Then heat sunflower margarine in a pan and add the dough for oval potato pancakes with a larger spoon. These let you roast from both sides golden brown. The tastes go by the way from golden yellow to crispy brown apart. Try it.

You can serve now! You can eat them with applesauce or sugar. But I always liked her best.

Good Appetite!

Updrögt beans

- Source www.Ostfrieseninfo.de

Something for the East Frisian "gourmets" and also one of the East Frisian national dishes. The beans (variety: "Hinrichs Giant" / "bacon beans") are pulled on a thread after harvesting and dried in the kitchen or on the rooftop to preserve the typical flavor.

500g beans, 500g potatoes, 500g bacon, 4 peeled sausages (Mettwürstchen), salt and pepper.

Soak the beans in plenty of water the day before, cut into pieces and cook in fresh water for about 30 minutes, then change the water, add the bacon and simmer for about 1-1.5 hours with a little salt. Now add potatoes and sausages, let it boil, add salt and possibly some vinegar with pepper - taste and pound

(or not).

Well, here is beer and the grain after that inevitable!

About Moa Graven

Moa Graven is an German writer of Crime Storys and was born in Ostfriesland Germany. She started writing Crime in year of 2013 at age over fifty years and now, she is living only for writing. It's a dream, she said. She lives with her husband und two lovely dos on nature land in East Frisian.

Visit her on www.moa-graven.de

The other books from Moa Graven (German)

Die Eva Sturm Krimi-Reihe im Überblick

Verliebt ... Verlobt ... Verdächtig - *Band 01*

Justitias Schwäche - *Band 02*

Bitterer Todesengel - *Band 03*

Blaues Blut - *Band 04*

Stille Angst - *Band 05 (Overcross-Special mit den drei ostfriesischen Ermittlerteams von Moa Graven, die einen Fall auf Borkum lösen)*

Schiffbruch - *Band 06*

Auf dich wartet der Tod - *Band 07*

7 Tage Regen – *Band 08*

Wenn es Abend wird, mein Schatz ... – *Band 09*

Stirb leise ... – *Band 10*

Der letzte Tanz – *Band 11*

Und alle haben geschwiegen – *Band 12*

Alle Bücher sind als eBook und Taschenbuch erhältlich!

Die weiteren Krimi-Reihen von Moa Graven

Kommissar Guntram Krimi-Reihe

Mörderischer Kaufrausch - Band 01

Mord im Gebüsch - Band 02

Mordsgeschäfte - Band 03

Das Meer schweigt ... - Band 04

Märchenhafte Morde - Band 05

Hinter verschlossenen Türen - Band 06

Teezeit - Band 07

Wer erschoss den Weihnachtsmann? - Band 08

Hannah – Vergessene Gräber - Band 09

297 Tage - Band 10

Tod einer Prinzessin - Band 11

Profiler Jan Krömer Krimi-Reihe

KillerFEE – Band 01

Todesspiel am Großen Meer – Band 02

Kneipenkinder – Band 03

Fallensteller - Band 04

Flächenbrand – Band 05

Blindgänger – Band 06

Fremder - Band 07

Die Puppenstube - Band 08

H.E.A.T.H.E.R – *Band 09*

Der Adler – Joachim Stein Krimi-Reihe
Der Adler – LaLeLu ... und tot bist du - Band 01
Der Adler - KALT - Band 02
Der Adler - NEBEL - Band 03
Der Adler - Lebenslänglich - Band 04
Der Adler – Der Nachbar – Band 05

Soko Norddeich 117 Krimi-Reihe
Wetterleuchten und ein Todesfall - Band 01

Alle Bücher sind als Taschenbuch oder eBook erhältlich!